THE ADVENTURES OF
LOLA

By Jade Harley

The Adventures Of Lola

First published in 2017
www.theadventuresoflola.com
ISBN 978-1542844871

Copyright © Jade Harley 2017

Cover art © Craig Phillips

Internal illustrations © Craig Phillips

This book is dedicated to Liam and Lana.

Be in love with the adventure of life.

ONE

MYSTERIOUS MR HOLT

Hi, my name is LOLA, and this is my story. They say everyone has at least one story in them and that it helps to make sense of your life if you write it down, in case you forget it later. So here I am, keeping a log of my life. I hope it will be a long life, filled with wonderful adventures that I can share with you.

Getting to Know Me ☺
I am thirteen going on 21 (or so I'm told).
I get myself into trouble ALL the time.
I love action, running, jumping, kicking, climbing things; you get the picture.
I LOVE big boots (easy to run, jump and kick things).
I am always changing my hair colour, it's bright blue right now, but last week it was bright pink.
I live in the beautiful Blue Mountains in Australia.
I'm going to be a world famous adventuress one day.
I am a BIG list writer, I even write lists about writing lists.
I have two amazing friends that stick by me no matter what.
I love all animals and insects, but especially butterflies and dragonflies.

So now that you know a little bit about me, you can a) choose to stick around or b) go back to whatever it was you were doing before you picked up this book...

Oh, you're sticking around; that's cool. I'll try and keep it interesting, let me know if I'm losing you.

Like most stories ever told by anyone ever, my story starts in a very ordinary setting. And what can be more ordinary than school?

I know school isn't *ALL* bad. There's some interesting stuff to learn and then there's lunchtime and playtime, and they totally count. But some of the lessons I have to sit through, well let's just say they seem designed to test my patience.

Reasons Why School Annoys Me ☹

All the teachers are old and smelly.
You have to sit still and be quiet for hours on end.
You **have** to go even if there's something much more fun on – like the fair!
The uniform is lame, I have to wear a skirt and I hate skirts.
You have to do homework and that gets in the way of my fun time.

I think that paints a pretty clear picture of why my school sucks. But I am getting sidetracked, back to the beginning of my story.

On this particular day in question, I was outside the Headmaster's office (don't ask) and I saw a new teacher arrive. Well, that's not so special I hear you reply...

Ah but that's my point. There are NEVER new teachers at my school, it's one of the reasons it's so dull. A new student is always fun and a new teacher might just liven the place up a bit. "New challenger awaits!" I can almost hear the call to arms.

He's definitely younger than the rest of them, with a full head of curly black hair instead of the usual wisps of grey or shiny bald top. This one seems to have a spring in his step and dare I say, a mischievous sparkle in his eyes. Oh glory be, at worst it's a semester's worth of fun breaking him in, and at best he might have epic tales to tell and actually be a FUN teacher.

So anyway, I'm sussing him out, whilst also pretending to write my lines...

I will not dance during lessons.
I will not dance during lessons.
I will not dance during lessons.
I will not dance during lessons.
I will not dance during lessons.
I will not dance during lessons.

I overheard a few garbled whispers from the new teacher. It was something along these lines:

"There's no need to panic. We can't _____ _____ know or there will be a mass evacuation. The last time this happened, it took years to build back ___ _____, and you know the trouble that caused. Anyway, it might just be a false alarm. I'm here to make sure everything is okay, but you need to keep it a secret. The _____ can't find out I'm here."

The Headmaster listened on impatiently and then replied. "I know why you're here and I'll tolerate you in my school if I must, but don't go spreading any silly rumours or getting the students all riled up. Now, I don't want to hear another word about it."

I don't know about you, but that got my alarm bells ringing. I was also feeling something else though. I was excited, I admit it. This sounded like action and I wanted in!! Just imagine, LOLA to the rescue. I didn't know what the new teacher was there for, but I was willing to bet he needed a trusty sidekick.

Praise the trees, could this be it? Could there really be a crisis of epic proportions (requiring a heroine) about to take place in my sleepy town? Feeling pretty sure that my detention and completion of lines would now be less important, I decided to sneak off to my next class and share the news with my bestest friends in the whole world

ALLIE and JET ☺☺

My friend Jet is super cool and super nerdy, and he's a whizz at anything technical. He's also a pretty decent ninja warrior. He has a spinning high kick that could knock your block off and no one messes with him. He doesn't say much, but when he does it's pretty deep and normally worth paying attention to. He has a really annoying habit of always being right, even when you'd like him to keep his opinions to himself, thank you very much! He's super protective and has always had my back 100%.

Allie is way girlier than me, but that's okay. She's super gorgeous, caring and funny and she's always looking out for us. She also does some pretty epic animal impressions; my favourite is her giraffe. Allie and I have been best friends forever and I tell her everything. She is the type of friend who will stick up for you no matter what. I can't imagine life without Allie and Jet.

As I ran into the classroom, I forgot in my excitement that it was Mr. Reacher's classical studies class. Yawn.

The boredom in the room was so thick you could cut a big chunk out of it. As I skidded through the door and tried to walk calmly, Mr. Reacher's dark stormy stare warned me that I was on thin ice. Taking my usual seat up the back of the class behind Allie and Jet, I made a supersized effort to look interested. When I was sure I wasn't being watched, I whispered to them what I'd overheard outside the Headmaster's office.

"You know what this means," said Jet.

"What?" I leaned in, keen to hear his wise words.

"I have absolutely no idea, you're missing all the important words," he deadpanned.

"But look at the words I did hear: 'there's no need to panic' or 'mass evacuation,' for example!" I couldn't quite understand why he was not taking this more seriously.

"LOLA, you can be such a drama queen sometimes," Jet sighed loudly.

"Playing devil's advocate here . . ." Allie, as always the peacekeeper, chimed in. "Maybe it will be okay? Whoever this new teacher is, he seems to think that now that he's here, it'll be alright."

"Well I think someone needs to get to the bottom of it. What happened before? That's what I really want to know," I replied, quite disappointed that my friends weren't as interested in this mystery as I was.

9

I knew that this was my destiny no matter what anyone thought. I just had a feeling. My instincts are usually pretty good and this could be the start of a great adventure. I was not willing to be put off, even by my best friends. Trouble was looming, I was sure of it.

The rest of the day passed in a blur of numbers and facts, facts and numbers. My head was on another planet. So much to uncover...

Who was this mysterious new teacher?

Why was he here now, and why was the Headmaster tolerating him?

More importantly, WHO were they keeping it a secret from?

What had happened before?

And how could I get to the bottom of it?

Oh it was so delicious to have so much going on in my brain. School was over and as I made my way home, a plan had started to form in my thoughts.

LOLA's Plan:

Make friends with the new teacher, find out who he is and where he comes from – need full background check and his likes/dislikes etc...

Write a list of ALL possible situations that would create a panic.

Prove to Jet and Allie that there really IS something going on and that I need their help.

By the time I arrived home, I felt pretty confident that whatever the issue was, I could save the day. Surely, once I'd established my new identity as 'epic adventuress, a.k.a. LOLA who saved the day,' I'd be able to travel the world going from one adventure to the next. My parents couldn't say no to that, now could they? If I succeeded, it didn't matter what stupid rules I was breaking.

As I arrived home, my head still buzzing with my grand plans, I was quickly brought back down to earth by the look on my Mum's face.

"LOLA I heard you were in detention today, AGAIN!"

"I was only dancing a little bit and the teacher was being really boring. You know I can't sit still for that long. Plus, I've heard that sitting at a desk for too long is bad for you," I replied. I knew I was pushing my luck, but I just couldn't resist.

My Mum sighed and smiled slightly despite herself. I knew she secretly quite enjoyed my feisty spirit (although she'd never admit it to my Dad).

"Well that may be true," she chuckled, "but you have to do what the teacher says in school, it's the rules. Sometimes I'd like to ignore the rules too, but we can't, so please, *for me*, can you try to stay still in class and pay attention?" She paused for a little while whilst I rolled my eyes.

"Okay, *just for you*," I replied with a cheeky grin. "You won't tell Dad will you?"

"Not this time, but don't push it missy."

I knew better than to answer her back and rushed up to my room. "Mum I've got homework to do, so please don't disturb me!" I cried as I flew upstairs. I heard her go back into the kitchen and knew I was safe to get cracking on my investigation.

JADE HARLEY

TWO

THE PLOT THICKENS

My room is awesome, my parents are pretty cool when it comes to letting me decorate. It's full of wicked plants and flowers, the walls are silver with wooden beams on the ceiling, and I have electric blue and purple bed covers. I just love it. When we first moved in, it was pretty I guess, but it lacked a certain pizazz and over time I've made it match my favourite colours. When I lie back in bed, I can gaze at the moon and the stars and the jet-black skies through a skylight above my bed. So hey, I'm not complaining.

I DID have homework, that part was true, but I had much more important things to attend to. I had to write my plan out on paper and do some research on major things that had happened in our town's history. I thought that would be a good place to start, as whatever IT was, IT seemed to have happened before.

The plan was no problem. I love a good list so I got that done in minutes. But when I started searching online for major things that had happened in the past 50 years, the most curious thing kept happening. I'd be searching and all the usual stuff would come up, births, deaths, weddings, so and so did this, so and so did that, stories of bravery and cute stuff about animals... but whenever I got to 1985 I'd get this message:

No records found...

Curious...

I tried all the daily papers and monthly magazines, even the Blue Mountains Herald, which has everything in it, no matter how small... and a similar message appeared.

There are no records that match your search...

Even weirder was this one...

Sorry, but nothing of interest happened in 1985.

Well now I was SURE there was something up! How could <u>nothing</u> have happened in 1985? It just didn't make any sense. After an hour of frustrated searching, I was called down to dinner. I decided to ask my parents about it, they were alive then, so they would surely know.

14

Dinner was always a pretty somber affair. My Dad was always fairly quiet when he got home from work, so my Mum fussed about him, trying to work out what kind of day he'd had and whether it was safe to start a lively conversation. Mum was a talker. Dad not so much.

"So darling, why don't you tell us about your day?" she asked me. Dad raised his head and his eyebrows, as if to imply, this should be interesting.

"Well..." I hesitated. "It's actually quite curious and I think you can help me uncover a great mystery!" I announced hopefully.

"Well that does sound interesting! If we can help, I'm sure we will. What's this great mystery that needs solving?" Mum nodded at Dad with a sly grin.

"You know you've lived here for like a *long* time... well I'm doing some research for a project I'm working on (wink wink) and I can't seem to find anything AT ALL that happened here in 1985!" My Dad turned red in the face and suddenly seemed uncomfortable in his chair.

"Huh," was all he managed to say. My Mum got up and busied herself at the kitchen sink.

"Well don't you both think that's weird? Surely SOMETHING must have happened that year and if it did, which it obviously had to, then why can't I read about it anywhere at all?" I asked them.

"I have no idea what you're talking about," my Dad replied, before staring back at his dinner. "What is this project you're working on anyway? Sounds like a waste of time to me."

"That's not very helpful Dad, I need to know about 1985, it's important!"

"How can the project be so important if you can't tell me what it is? Sounds to me like you're looking for trouble, and I have a mind to go into that school and find out what's going on," he was getting redder and redder in the face.

"Now now Francis, don't go getting yourself all worked up, I'm sure LOLA can find something else to do her project on, can't you LOLA?" Mum seemed to want me to stop talking. So I did just that. I planned to keep investigating, but clearly I wouldn't be getting any answers from them! Typical.

I had a restless night's sleep. I tossed and turned, but no matter how I rationalized things, I couldn't shake the feeling that there WAS a mass cover up and that it WAS going to happen again. Whatever IT was!

Reasons for a Possible Cover Up:

1. Criminal activity at the highest levels of the land
2. Alien invasion
3. The world ends and this is a new world (like the dinosaurs, sort of?)
4. Humans find out about us and we are all experimented on for science

Wait.
Stop.
Rewind.
Hang on a minute, I hear you cry.
What was that last one?
Oh yes, sorry I forgot to mention. We are FAIRIES.

THREE

FAIRIES DON'T EXIST

I know what you're thinking. Fairies don't exist! Well I'm proof that we do.

My kind have lived on this earth much longer than you have. We lived in harmony with nature and alongside the dinosaurs, we survived the asteroid that crashed into the earth and wiped the dinosaurs out, and yes—we still exist today.

Well, why don't you see us? *Fair enough question.*

It's simple. You don't really look that closely.

From a distance, we look similar to dragonflies or butterflies, so we normally fly by undetected. We live in very secluded parts of the earth and try to stay away from humans as much as possible. We are so small, and we move so quickly, that you have to look very carefully to spot us.

Facts about Fairies – True or False?

1. Fairies can fly.
TRUE. But we don't fly all the time; we stay mostly on the ground during the day and come out to play at sunrise and sunset.

2. Fairies glow.
TRUE. We glow for practical reasons so we can find each other at night or in our underground homes. We only glow when we feel very sure that there are no humans nearby.

3. Fairies can change their bodies and appearance.
TRUE. It's called *Glimmering*. We can change our appearance to look like insects and small birds. We look very similar to butterflies and dragonflies, so we normally choose to make ourselves look just like them when we are anywhere near humans.

4. Fairies are very fast.
TRUE. We move very quickly and we can switch direction easily, it helps us to stay unseen by humans.

5. Fairies can grant wishes.
TRUE. But only if it is in harmony with nature. If you ask to win the lotto or get a new toy, we can't help you with that, but if you make a true wish that is pure of heart and we hear it, we can choose to grant that wish.

6. Fairies can heal.
TRUE. We do have the power to heal some wounds, but we cannot save someone who is dying. Nature involves life and death and we are in tune with nature.

7. Fairies are immortal.
UNTRUE. Fairies are semi-mortal, which means we can heal each other's wounds. Just like humans, if we are mortally wounded and our life force is broken, we return back to nature.

8. Fairies can communicate with animals.
TRUE. We can speak to insects, birds and animals. If nature is threatened or we need help outside of our community, we can ask for their help.

9. Fairies haunt houses.
UNTRUE. We stay away from humans as a general rule. We live mainly in small communities and stick to ourselves. There are the odd loner fairies that sometimes live in towns and villages, but they are very rare, and we haven't heard of any living in people's houses. The risk of capture would be far too great. These are more likely to be *Brownies*, another form of magical creature but not a fairy; they love humans and housework and often live with people. They are quite harmless, and very good at disguise. Lastly, they only come out at night and can't be spotted, but you might notice that your kitchen is clean in the morning. Leave them out some sweets or honey to say thanks and they will live quite happily with you.

10. Fairies snatch human babies.
UNTRUE and quite honestly ridiculous. What would we want to steal a human baby for? This myth has given us a bad name over the years and it is quite upsetting to us. We love children and would never do anything to hurt them.

11. There are many types of fairies.
TRUE. Actually, there *were* many types of fairies, but most have died out or live so remotely that even WE don't know whether or not they still exist. The four main types of fairies still living in large numbers across the world are:
Forest Fairies
Little People
Mountain Fairies (that's us!)
Water Fairies

12. The best time to see a fairy is at sunrise or sunset.
TRUE, but we will *only* show ourselves to children who truly believe in us and who have a great love of animals and nature. If you suspect there is a fairy living near you, the best thing to do is be especially kind to animals and wildlife. We are always watching and on rare occasions, we will show ourselves to someone special. If you are protecting nature from pollution or other destructive forces of the human world, you may well be chosen. If this happens, we will glow a golden light to show ourselves and illuminate our tiny bodies beneath our beating wings. We'll also hover in one spot for longer than usual. If this happens you have just seen a fairy!
I'm assuming that if you're reading this book, you're not a full-fledged adult yet and your mind and imagination are still open to the idea of magic and fairies. If you look hard enough at the next dragonfly or butterfly you see, you might just spot our little bodies and our big piercing eyes. If you do spot a fairy, you must keep us a secret from adults! If they found out about us, they'd want to cut us open and experiment on us. I'd prefer not to be experimented on, if you don't mind.

So now I've shared the truth about our world. Can I trust you to keep our secret?

FOUR

MISSION ACCEPTED

I woke up with a nasty feeling that my suspicions were true. In 1985, something **must** have happened to expose us to the humans, and something terrible must have resulted from it.

What else could it be?

Determined to get to the bottom of things, I headed into school with one goal in mind: Make friends with the new teacher and get him to spill the beans.

With everything on my mind, it was harder than usual to concentrate, but I had to appear calm, well behaved and keen to learn for the new teacher. This was important to my plan, and I couldn't afford to make a bad impression when so much was at stake!

As it turns out, I didn't have to wait long at all to meet him. I walked into my homeroom and took my usual spot, ready to chime out my name when called.

"LOLA," I heard, but it wasn't Mrs. Macc doing role call today, it was none other than the NEW teacher. *Where's Mrs. Macc?* I thought, but I quickly shut my mouth before the words escaped. Teachers don't generally like questions, and remember, I'm trying to win him over.

I merely replied, "Here sir," and smiled brightly. He seemed satisfied and moved on to the rest of the class. Without any prompting from me, he told the class that Mrs. Macc had been called away on family matters and that he was filling in for the foreseeable future. Foreseeable, eh? That meant that whatever IT was, he was planning to stick it out until IT was fixed. I took that to be a good sign!

The rest of home class went by without incident.

As we were headed out to our first class - Maths (yuck!), I decided to take a risk and ask a question that I thought might tell me whether I was onto something or not.

"Sir? Is it true that humans, outside of some children, don't know that we exist?" My question was innocent enough, I thought, as this was common knowledge amongst fairies.

"Yes LOLA, that is true. Most humans can't imagine a world outside of their own and are therefore happy to see us as part of the animal world," he replied.

"Well, what would happen if they did know?" I was risking it now, but I had to press him.

"Well LOLA, I'm sure I have no idea, but we are very careful so it won't ever happen. Why are you asking?" He was getting curious now, I could tell.

"No reason Sir, just something I heard on the grapevine," I replied, as if it was just an innocent question.

"Well, why don't you focus on your studies and ignore silly rumours. As I said, humans think we are part of the animal world and that's the way it will stay as long as everyone follows the rules," he replied, ending the conversation and making his way briskly to his next class.

First attempt at contact not too bad, I thought, he hadn't gotten too cross with me. But he also hadn't told me anything new. I KNEW there was more to it. So throughout the day, I decided to ask all my teachers the same question. No matter who I asked, I got the same reply: "LOLA, humans don't know about us and that's the way it will stay, now focus on your work please!" It was like they were all reading from the same script.

The day dragged on. I wasn't going to see Allie and Jet again until lunch break, so by the time I saw them, I was bursting to tell them everything I'd discovered so far. Not much, I know, but it WAS suspicious and they could no longer ignore that.

Jet was busy doing somersaults on the playground when I found him, with Allie quietly drawing by his side.

"Guys, remember what I told you I overhead yesterday outside the Headmaster's office?" I asked them.

"Yes," they replied in unison.

"Well last night, I started doing some research. I thought I'd check back over the last 50 years to see if anything came up, like some kind of disaster or panic-inducing event. Guess what I found?" I almost shouted with excitement.

"NO idea," they both answered.

"Absolutely nothing at all happened in 1985!" I cried.

"Well that's no real surprise," said Jet. "Nothing much happens around here, we know that already."

"Don't you see—that's my point. There are heaps of things written for all the other years, all the usual stuff like people getting married, having babies, school fetes and events etc... But in 1985 absolutely NOTHING happened. Isn't that the most curious thing?"

"Are you sure you were looking properly? If that is true, then it would be weird..." said Jet. "But you must have been doing it wrong. Let me have a go."

I could tell I had his attention now. Allie looked on, puzzled.

"Let's go to the library and check it out together," suggested Jet and off he flew, Allie and I buzzing behind him and trying desperately to keep up.

The library was my favourite place in the school, (apart from the being quiet bit), because it was full of the most awesome books and we were pretty much left alone to do what we wanted. We logged into the main computer (yes fairies have computers too, we're up on all modern technology you know) and Jet started entering in some searches.

First he typed in *'History of 1985.'* Sure enough, he was met with the same reply as me...

There are no records that match your search.

Both Jet and Allie looked at each other in confusion, and then looked at me strangely. I gave them a knowing nod and said, "I told you I wasn't making it up, it's weird right?"

"Hmm," said Jet, "that is strange. Okay, let's try something less obvious..."

'1985 births and deaths' he tried next.

There are no records that match your search.

26

THE ADVENTURES OF LOLA

"Okay this is getting really spooky, how can no one have been born or died in 1985?" asked Allie.

"It's not possible, I said. **Someone** is covering **something** up, I just know it. Now do you believe me?" I was desperate for them to agree, I needed their help.

"Let's not jump to any conclusions, BUT let's just say that there IS a cover up. I'm not saying that it's bad just yet, BUT I'm willing to admit that this is getting suspicious. What's your theory?" asked Jet.

I was so relieved that they were finally taking me seriously, that I began to spout off all my dramatic theories about aliens and government cover ups, criminal activity, and I ended with the big one—that the humans HAD in fact found out about us fairies, in a big way, and that there had been some kind of disaster in the Blue Mountains as a result.

I still wasn't 100% sure what the disaster might be, but I told them about how I'd questioned the teachers and my parents and how everyone seemed to give the same frustrating answer. Therefore, I was positive that I was onto something and it wasn't good!

Phew! I was so excited, scared and yet happy that my friends believed me. I'd forgotten to breath and had been circling furiously in the air, buzzing from one plant to the next in my excitement.

"Calm down LOLA, you'll make yourself dizzy," urged Allie. Allie hadn't said much so far, I could tell she was thinking it all through.

"So the big question, LOLA, is what do we do about this? If no one is talking, and the new teacher is here to stop it from happening again, how can WE do anything? It seems like we just have to wait and see," she told me.

"But I feel like I found all this out for a reason," I replied.

I don't know why I felt so certain about this, but I just did. It was my destiny, I was SURE of it!

"First things first," said Jet. "Lets just think this through. Let's say, LOLA, that you are right and something bad DID happen in 1985. We're all here now, right? Our parents and teachers lived through it, so it can't have been that bad. We fly past humans unseen all the time and nothing has ever happened, has it?" he asked sensibly.

"Yes that's true, but…"

"No buts LOLA, we need to think clearly and deal with the facts. Whatever happened, it must have been fixed, because we are here and not in test tubes. So, let's try and speak to someone who was alive in 1985. It can't be a teacher or a parent, it needs to be someone else, someone no one would think of talking to," he said.

"I know!" exclaimed Allie. "How about the caretaker, he must be at least 70 and he's lived here all his life. Everyone thinks he's mad, so no one really talks to him, but I've heard he was once an explorer and even went to Borneo to meet with exotic fairy tribes over there. If that's true, maybe he will know something?"

"That's actually a great idea Allie!" I cried.

The caretaker was quite a mystery to us. It was rumoured that he spent his early years flying from country to country meeting with fairy folk and finding out about their customs and special powers. But everyone knew that the King didn't allow travel, so I wasn't sure how that could actually be true. There were other rumours that he had a wife and a child once, but none of this was ever confirmed and he lived alone. So, if he did have a wife and a child, where did they go? He was quite grumpy, so we tended to stay away from him.

But for lack of any better ideas, we all agreed that meeting with him was worth a try. If the rumours were true about him being an explorer, there was a chance he knew something…

FIVE

TALES FROM THE CARETAKER

The bell rang for the end of lunch break and we promised to meet after school and find the caretaker.

How I sat through the rest of my classes without bursting, I have no idea. I was such a jumble of nerves. To be honest, the caretaker freaked me out a bit, he always looked so moody and mean. But the thought that he might know what happened in 1985 was enough to make me face my fears, after all, how bad could he be? When the bell rang for the end of class, I flew off at lightening speed to meet Jet and Allie at the gates. They arrived shortly after and we quickly came up with a plan.

"LOLA, you do the talking, and we'll back you up. Remember, the idea is not to spook him or make him mad. We need to show genuine interest in his adventures and see if we can make him drop his guard. Let him do the talking, old people love to talk if you ask the right questions. Maybe he's lonely, who knows? Let's try and make a friend today, agreed?"

"Agreed," I replied.

The caretaker lived in an underground house at the back of the school grounds. It was very run down, but it had a certain lived in charm to it. It was nestled into the foot of the mountains under the roots of a huge eucalyptus tree, with rocky peaks and dark green trees standing proudly in the background.

As we approached, we could see him pottering around, he looked so frail in the dim light, his greying wings were almost see through. He must have heard us approach, because he turned sharply to face our direction and scowled fiercely. I went from feeling sorry for him one minute to being very scared the next.

Jet and Allie shoved me forward and I found myself face to face with him, not quite sure where to begin.

"Well," he said, "what are you lot doing here, don't you have homes to go to or parents to annoy?"

"Sir, well the thing is..." I mumbled, tripping over my words and fidgeting. "We've heard you were once a brave and adventurous explorer, and well, I'd like to be an adventuress one day, and I was hoping you might give me some tips?"

Pretty rubbish start, but it was the best I could come up with on the spot. He scowled at me and stared so deeply into my eyes that I thought my head would explode. Then something strange happened. His face softened and his scowl melted away. He looked off into the distance, for what felt like forever, before he turned to me and whispered.

"Well now, it's been a long time since anyone asked me anything about that. Everyone steers clear of me you know; they call me names behind my back. Why aren't you lot scared of me?" He seemed genuinely interested.

"I don't believe in being scared of anyone Sir, not if I'm going to be a world famous adventuress," I replied, with way more confidence than I actually felt.

"Well good for you," he said, "there's nothing to be gained by living a life in fear. I was like you once, before that..." his words trailed off and it was clear that we were losing him to his memories.

Jet chimed in, "Sir would you tell us about your adventures please, we'd love to hear them and we promise we won't tell anyone!"

Both Allie and I nodded our heads furiously in agreement. "Well you'd better come inside then, it's getting a bit nippy out here and I can't handle the cold like I used to," he sighed sadly.

We followed him into his dimly lit yet charming little house. It really was quite warm and snug inside, and like most fairy houses, the front door was just a raised opening under a mound of grass. Below ground, it opened up into an underground house - not unlike the ones that humans live in, but just under your feet.

As we found a place to sit, the caretaker paced back and forth, seemingly unsure about where to start.

"Can you tell us about when you went to Borneo?" I suggested. "I heard that you once met with forest fairies. Is that true?"

31

This made him smile. In fact he seemed to glow just for a second and I could almost see the young fairy he once was emerge from behind the deep wrinkles and sagging face of old age.

"Oh I didn't just meet them young miss, I lived with them in the forest for over a year!"

"Really, but I thought that was against the law, how did you get away with it?" I was surprised and excited by his answer. It is a well-known fact that the King has banned any travel outside of our town, unless you receive a special pass from him for Royal matters of security. Even to visit other fairies is strictly forbidden, in case it alerts humans to our existence. And you are certainly not allowed to LIVE with them; you'd be captured and arrested!

"It wasn't always that way, you see...," he said sadly. "Years ago when there were fewer people and more fairies, we moved around a lot more freely. Now we have all these rules and laws, stuff and nonsense. I say, what will be will be!"

Curious, could this be a clue? I decided to risk it and press him for more details...

"So what you're saying is that the rules we've been told are the LAW, have only really come about in the last few years. How many years would you say sir?"

"Well I'd say it would have to be around... let me think. Time goes by so quickly these days..."

I tried to keep my face calm as the caretaker racked his brain.

"Ah well, I'm 72 now and I stopped travelling around 30 odd years ago. Yes, that sounds about right. That's when it became the law, and until then it was more of a guideline. I've never been much for rules but erm... these were crazy times and well, things happened. Bad things. Things I'd prefer not to go into if you don't mind." He seemed to snap back into character at this point, and I saw again the sad, scowled face of a fairy that had seen too much, known too much pain.

I didn't want to push it, but this might be our one chance, I just had to ask. I decided to take a chance.

"Do you mean in 1985, when the humans found out about us and terrible things happened that the powers that be covered up?" I held my breath waiting to see his reaction. Allie and Jet both gasped slightly, I don't think they were expecting me to be so bold.

"What do you know about that? What is this, some kind of test? Well I won't tell you, you won't hear it from me. I'm an old man and some things are best left buried." He sat down gruffly in his seat and I knew we were losing him.

I tried one last time. This was it I thought, no point holding back now.

"It's going to happen again, Sir, and only we can stop it. You need to help us. Tell us what happened so it doesn't happen again," I begged him. I knew now, more than ever, that this was real and that he had BEEN there, I just had to get him to tell us what had happened.

"What do you mean it's going to happen again? We're much more careful now, all these new rules and laws are supposed to protect us. Why do you say this, why are you trying to upset an old man? I've heard enough, I'd like you to leave now please." He was really upset now and although I wanted to question him some more, both Allie and Jet moved me towards the door and I knew I'd gotten all I was going to get that night.
Just before we headed outside, I quickly broke free of my friends and darted back inside the house.

"Sir, one last question and I promise that we'll leave you in peace... I can't leave without knowing, or it will eat me up. Did the humans find out about us and did they capture some of us for experiments? Is that what all the secrecy is about?"

"Oh dear me, I can see you're a pushy one," he replied with a strange mix of amusement and sadness on his face. "If you must know, it was much, much worse. Yes the humans found out about us, but they didn't just capture us, they destroyed our entire community. Only a handful of fairies survived, it was the worst event in our history and we all lost so much. It took years to rebuild and we've never been the same since, in my opinion."

I was stunned. I wasn't expecting this honesty at all. I admit that a tiny part of me was happy that I was right, but I had also been secretly hoping that I would be wrong. How did something this big happen in our community without anyone talking about it afterward? Why was it wiped from all public record? Surely, we have a right to know?!

"It all happened so fast and none of us saw it coming, I was away on a short trip at the time, meeting with a fairy tribe in the desert. I was on my way back home, when the entire animal kingdom sounded the alarm. I've never heard such a racket - every animal joined in chorus to warn of trouble in the hills of the Blue Mountains.

I flew as fast and as hard as I could. I gathered others along the way who had also heard the calls, but by the time we got there, it was too late. The destruction was terrifying. Homes upturned, great holes in the rocks and trees uprooted to reveal our underground homes. White plastic domes over entire areas and thousands of our community pinned down on the ground or stuck to the sides of the domes unable to move or break free.

Inside were men and women in white suits and masks carrying clipboards, making notes and putting fairies into tubes and bags. It was so clinical, so inhuman. I don't understand how humans can live with themselves. This belief that they are the superior beings, when we fairies and animals have been here for way longer than they have and done far less damage!" he was shouting now, his face red with anger.

"I tried with all my might to break through the domes and help everyone. Most of my friends were dead or dying, but some were still trying to escape. I couldn't understand how so many had gotten captured. We are quick and nimble, I thought, but it was so unexpected and so swift that when the trucks rolled in and the domes went down, most fairies were caught completely unaware. They didn't raise the alarm until it was too late..." His voice wavered off as he was transported back in time to face the horrible events again.

I understood now all those lessons and lectures we'd been taught at school and at home. Why we NEVER show ourselves to adult humans no matter how kind to nature they may appear to be. How only a very few special children, who are responsible for extraordinary acts of kindness to the animal and natural world, are ever allowed to see us. And most importantly, why we stay out of cities and towns where humans live in the thousands.

We sat dumbstruck as the caretaker continued to tell of fairies of all ages taken away and experimented on. From a community of over 3,000 fairies, only a few hundred had survived and these were fairies who were not at home that day - either travelling or just outside of the community. One school group escaped the devastation as they were on a field trip that day. A number of our current teachers were on that trip, and our King and Queen were also spared as they were visiting New Zealand on Royal duties.

When the survivors returned, they decided to rebuild the community in a much more remote location. It was decided by Royal decree that the events that took place in 1985, and all information about the rebuild of the community and the new location, would be wiped from the record books to protect us. New strict laws were put in place by the King to ban travel in and out of the area, anything to keep us safe from humans. The King blamed the disaster on the large amount of fairies flying into and out of the area; he claimed that this attracted the human attention, so it became a crime to leave the area without permission from the King.

Now that we knew the truth, I almost wished that we didn't. If this could happen again, how on earth could we stop it? We'd need to know who was planning it, and when they'd be coming. It was too much to take in. We thanked the caretaker for telling us, and promised him that we'd keep it secret so he wouldn't get into any trouble. We had one piece of the puzzle – the past. What we needed now was the next piece of the puzzle – the future.

As we headed home, the dusk light was fading and I knew another sleepless night lay ahead.

NO I WON'T WEAR THAT

Saturday is the best day of the week by far. The weekend has just started, and that means no school and I have a weekly mixed martial arts class with Jet. To say we love it is an understatement.

As I head off to gym today, I have mixed emotions. Part of me feels like I should be doing something more useful, but the other part of me is filled with anger and needs to kick something!

As it's Saturday and there's no school, this means I can't talk to the new teacher so I decide to focus on my training. They won't know what hit them. When I get to the gym, Jet is already in the ring, practicing his takedowns on some poor unworthy challenger. I bounce on my toes and start off with some stretching to warm up. I decide to do a few fast laps around the trees of the gym and Jet swoops in from nowhere to race me.

He's so fast it takes all I have to keep up, but I'm nothing if not competitive, so I dig deep and put all my heart and soul into it, channeling all the fear and mixed emotions of the past few days. Jet switches direction and flies straight up into the air like a rocket and I'm a millisecond behind, determined to catch him. I get just within reach as he turns and grins. He grabs me and we corkscrew back down to the gym, creating a mini whirlwind in our wake. We land with a thud on the gym floor and the coach is quick to pull us into line.

"You two stop fooling around, time to do your drills. You're holding up the class, again..." he's trying to look stern, but he has a slight grin that gives him away. Coach Fuller is awesome, it's hard to really make him mad, but every now and again he has to pretend to be cross.

With the stress and the uncertainty of the last few days, this is just the distraction we need. By training our bodies so hard, there is no room left for thinking and it's a welcome break.

We go head to head.

I catch Jet with an awesome upper cut, and he attacks back with his famous spinning head kick, but I catch his leg and tackle him to the ground. I've got him pinned to the ground for at least five seconds before he flips me over and holds me in a headlock. I tap out, defeated for this round but ready to win the next one. After an hour of serious no holds barred sparring in the ring, we are both exhausted and collapse in a heap. We lie panting on the mats as coach comes over to us.

"I don't know what has happened to you both since last week. You were great before, best in the class without a doubt, but today you were both on fire. Excellent work, keep it up champs!" Coach taps us both on the shoulders and we smile to each other. If only he knew, we think, if only he knew.

After class, Jet and I decided to head over to Allie's house to see what she was up to. We were pretty sure we'd find her in her room hard at work on some new creation or other. She had a pretty epic wardrobe. Even though I'm not always into her colour choices, you can't knock her creativity.

She wants to open a fashion boutique when she finishes school, and I'm pretty certain she'll do just that. She's certainly got the talent. She's made most of my outfits since we've known each other, and she even has a few paying clients! Her parents let her do the odd one for pocket money, but mostly she has to turn them away due to school and homework, so I feel pretty lucky that she makes my wardrobe for free.

I'm pretty fussy in the clothing department and Allie knows me better than anyone. If it were up to my Mum, I'd be wearing frilly skirts and puffy dresses, yuck. My Mum and I DO NOT share the same sense of style, but luckily Allie keeps me well supplied and my Mum doesn't get a choice. I prefer leggings and trousers any day of the week, they are much more practical than a dress!

As we suspected, when we knock on Allie's window she's hard at work at her desk. She has a bundle of silk and threads and some lacy stuff coiled around her feet and what looks like a rainbow-coloured dress that's nearly finished.

We knock on the window. She jumps and spins around, and then when she sees us both, she grins widely.

"Well hi you guys, I was just in middle of making a dress for tonight. I thought I'd try a hippie look, what do you think?" she twirls around holding the dress up against herself and flitting one way and then the other. Now that it's held up, I can see it's actually quite stunning and will certainly suit her tiny frame and big green eyes.

"Looks great Allie, but what do you mean tonight, where are you off to?" I ask.

"LOLA," cries Allie in shock, "you haven't forgotten about tonight have you?" Both Jet and I look at each other questioningly and then in unison turn to her and admit that we have no idea what she's talking about.

"Wow, it's only the first dance of the season, everyone will be there. We've been planning this for months and I've made you both outfits!" she sighs.

In all the excitement and worry of the last few days, I'd completely forgotten about the dance and it seemed Jet had too. To be fair, Allie was far more excited about the dance than either of us were. She loved nothing more than a good get together.

I didn't mind them, the music was normally cool and it was a chance to blow off some steam. But I knew Jet actively avoided them at all costs. Allie wasn't going to let us off the hook though.

"You know, everyone will be there tonight. It might be a good opportunity to do some detective work. In fact I'm sure the new teacher will be coming, it will be his first public appearance." Allie knew that we couldn't resist the opportunity to talk to him outside of school and she was right.

"Allie you've got me there," I said, "Jet, that means you are coming too I'm afraid, no excuses. Don't worry, we won't make you dance with doting Delta." I chuckled to myself. Jet's face turned red.

"Yeah good one," he snapped back. Delta was the bane of Jet's life. She'd had a crush on him for years and every chance she got, she tried to single him out. No matter how much he ignored her, she kept persisting. There's actually nothing wrong with Delta, outside of her blind love for Jet, but he is 100% not interested and he doesn't mind telling her so. Poor girl.

To lighten the mood, Allie decided to show us our outfits. Jet was first to try his on and he seemed happy with his all black number with loose ninja pants. I must admit, when he put it on he looked pretty awesome. The top was tight and made out of some type of plastic looking material, so it gleamed in the light like dark oil. His pants were big and baggy and tied round his ankles. When he outstretched his jet-black wings, he was quite a sight!

"Thanks Allie, not bad at all," he replied as he started doing shadow boxing in the corner.

Allie sighed dramatically and went back to her wardrobe. She knew that was all the praise she'd be getting from Jet, but the fact that he was wearing the outfit and showing off in the mirror meant he really liked it.

When Allie returned with my outfit, I was stunned.

It was a crazy emerald green number, with what looked like peacock feathers sewn into the top and wide black pants that were cropped at the knees to look like a skirt. I squeezed into the top and pulled on the pants, doing a little jig. Thank goodness she didn't make me a yucky dress! She knew me well enough to understand that anything frilly and pretty is likely to make me say, "No I won't wear that!" This was pure genius, pants that look like a skirt. My Mum would be happy. "Technically" I am wearing a skirt, but practically, I can still run and jump and fly like a demon.

"Great job Allie, this is perfect," I beamed.

"Oh it's just a little something I knocked together, no trouble at all," she said, downplaying her efforts. I knew she'd probably been working on the outfits after school for weeks on end, so I gave her a big hug and nudged Jet to do the same.

"So now we're all kitted up, what's the plan for tonight?" I asked.

"The dance starts at 7 p.m., so let's say we meet here at around 6 p.m. to get changed. We can head off together and hide outside in the trees. We'll watch who goes in and get a lay of the land, what do you think?" whispered Allie excitedly.

"Sounds like a plan," I replied. "I'll see you both back here at 6." With that, Jet and I raced off home.

In a few hours, we might get our chance to talk to the teacher, where should we start? Would he turn out to be friend or foe?

THE SUPER STRENGTH OF
THOMAS HOLT

At 6 p.m. on the dot, Jet and I arrived at Allie's place. Surprise surprise, she wasn't quite ready and asked us to wait outside while she applied a glimmer to herself. She wanted to try out new wings and colouring for tonight to match her dress and knowing Allie, as we do, believe me, this was probably about the tenth set of wings she'd glimmered.

After what seemed like forever, but was probably more like 15 minutes, Allie finally appeared and she looked stunning! Her wings were a beautiful fine silver, as was her body, and at the tips of her wings she had added all the colours of the rainbow to match her new dress.

"You look beautiful Allie," I exclaimed, knowing that despite her obvious beauty she still needed her best friend to tell her.

"Thanks LOLA, and you both look amazing as well! Oh I can't wait, tonight will be such fun and I've been practicing all my moves and my spins..."

"Come on you two, at this rate we'll be late. I thought you wanted to watch everyone enter, LOLA?" asked Jet and he was quite right. We had to remain vigilant and not get carried away by the fun of it all. We now knew that there was likely to be a real threat to the community, and we had to get to the bottom of it and stop it before it happened. Tonight could get us one step closer to knowing *who* was planning *what*, and more importantly *when*!

Jet sped off towards the gorge where the dance was taking place, high up in the mountains by Wentworth Falls. The gorge has a beautiful waterfall surrounded by deep forests and huge trees. It's a magical spot and though popular during the day for hikers, it is rarely visited by humans at night, making it the perfect hideaway for a large fairy gathering. A big fallen tree made the perfect venue with its huge roots and strong sturdy branches forming a perfect canopy over the forest floor.

As we approached, we could see the telltale signs of fairy activity. Low amber lights flickered in the distance, a foggy haze masked the whole area (which is a sure sign that a glimmer has been applied to hide us) and the air was pungent with eucalyptus and jasmine blossom. The sound of laughter and music increased as we got closer, meaning that many fairies were already inside. We took our position to the right of the waterfall, hovering in the tree line, and watched as hundreds of our friends and neighbours entered the dance.

They all looked dazzling in their best outfits, everyone had made a huge effort and it was quite a sight to behold. Even the teachers had smartened themselves up. Gone were the shabby brown and blue tired old outfits, replaced by fancy black and white wings with brilliant red-spotted vests.

Yet, so far there was no sign of the new teacher... Maybe he wasn't coming after all?

Bored with hanging around, I decided it was best to get in there and start our investigation. If the new teacher wasn't coming, well there was no point in missing the opportunity to dig a little with the other teachers. If the Headmaster was aware of the imminent danger, then in all likelihood he wasn't the only one.

"So here's the plan, let's split up and try to eavesdrop on some conversations between the Headmaster and the other teachers. We'll each take one side of the room and meet up later to share what we've heard," I instructed Allie and Jet. They both nodded in agreement and I was about to zip off when Allie quickly grabbed my foot and pulled me to a sharp stop.

"LOLA?" asked Allie hesitantly. "What happens if we hear something we don't like? We should have a safe word..."

"A safe word?" I asked

"Yes, some kind of word or gesture to signal that we need to meet and talk ASAP," added Allie, getting quite carried away with the whole thing. Hmm, I hadn't thought of that...

"Good point, let's just agree to meet back here in an hour. If it's urgent, then ask the DJ to play 'I've got a feeling' by the Black Eyed Bees, and that will be our cue to meet here immediately. Okay?" That seemed to satisfy Allie and off we flew, into the twinkling dance hall under the fallen tree canopy.

Inside, it was as magical as we expected. There were fireflies flitting around the canopy casting a wonderful amber light down onto the forest floor. A space had been cleared as a dance floor, and there was a honey dew fountain cascading at the far end near the DJ. The tables were covered in vines and ferns, making them look like part of the undergrowth. There was water cascading down the rocks at both sides, creating a mini waterfall effect and adding to the charm. Mushrooms of all varieties and sizes provided seating for the dance weary and there was a spotted slip and slide into the waterfall for the younger fairies to enjoy. It was breath taking.

I reminded myself that we were on a mission and that I could enjoy the festivities later. I made my way straight over to a huge pine where I could see the Headmaster talking to Mrs. Price, the Fine Arts teacher. I quite like Mrs. Price. As far as teachers go, she's definitely one of the better ones. She doesn't automatically seat me in the back row (most other teachers do!) and she seems to understand my need to get up and stretch my legs every now and again. She even lets us do our art lessons out in the field sometimes, which is awesome. And I get pretty good grades, which keeps my Mum and Dad happy.

They seemed to be having quite a lively chat, so I slipped in next to them and pretended to fiddle with my bootlaces. They didn't seem to notice me and continued talking.

"So what is his story then, Headmaster? This new chap, Thomas I think he's called, is that right?" asked Mrs. Price. Bingo, she's asking about the new teacher!! I could hardly believe my luck.

"Yes that's right, Thomas Holt is his name. He seems like a fine enough fellow. He won't be here for long though, just until Mrs. Macc has tied up her family issues." So he was sticking to that story then, was he? Luckily Mrs. Price was having none of it.

New Information Learned:

1. According to Mrs. Price, there was nothing wrong with Mrs. Maccs' family, so that was clearly suspicious!
2. The other teachers were definitely not in on whatever IT was, and the Headmaster didn't seem to think he needed to share IT with anyone.
3. Mr. Holt was here to do something secret that only HE could do – what could it be?
4. The King was not aware that Mr. Holt was a new teacher at the school – why the secrecy?

Hmm, the plot was thickening. Did this mean that the Headmaster was taking the new teacher (I now knew his name was Thomas Holt) seriously? And why didn't he want the King to know about him, surely if there WAS a threat to our community, the King should have been warned?

I was more confused than ever.

Not satisfied with what I had learned so far, I decided to do a quick lap of the party and try and spot Mr. Holt. He wasn't hard to find. Mr. Holt was dancing up a storm with a beautiful fairy I had never seen before. Maybe it was his wife or his girlfriend?

The whole room was watching as he twirled her this way then that, throwing her across the room like a professional dancer. He stopped suddenly and looked up, leaving her twirling off into the distance. He seemed to hear something and he bolted out of the door. I spotted Jet in quick pursuit of him and decided to make chase as well.

As I passed through the doorway of a thousand fireflies, I spotted Mr. Holt and Jet far ahead of me skimming up the waterfall. They were so fast, it was hard to keep them in my sight. Then I saw them crouched over a wild pig who had somehow got herself stuck in the roaring swell of the waterfall bank.

"Her legs are trapped under a fallen log!" screamed Jet above the sounds of the cascading water. "LOLA, go and get help, this is a job for at least ten fairies. Bring the strongest team you can find, quick, her head is slipping under the water." Jet was panicking, which was not like him. I rushed back to the dance to raise the alarm.

By the time I had returned with ten of the strongest fairies I could find - including our gym coach and three of the wrestling team - I saw the poor pig shaking and gasping for breath on the sodden grass to the side of the waterfall. Her hind legs were wounded but it was nothing we couldn't fix.

Jet was looking on stunned.

Mr. Holt jumped straight up and insisted that she was fine, no need to panic, she'd gotten her legs stuck but the force of the water had shifted it and all was now well. Relieved, everyone marveled at how the pig had gotten separated from her mother at such a late hour, and it was agreed that we would send a Messenger Fairy to find her mother and bring her here to care for her young one. Satisfied that the drama was over, everyone headed back to the dance. Jet and I agreed to stay back and wait for her mother to arrive.

As soon as everyone had gone and we were alone, Jet whispered urgently to me.

"That pig did not free itself. I'm telling you now, that teacher is not a normal teacher."

"What do you mean, what happened?" I'd never seen Jet rattled like this before.

"I've seen some pretty strong fairies in my time, but I've never seen one as strong as him. I think he might be a Protector!" exclaimed Jet. Protector Fairies were rumoured to be specially trained with extraordinary strength and magical skills. They were very rare and they tended to be loners, normally living near cities where it was more dangerous for fairies and animals in general to live alongside humans. I was doubtful that Mr. Holt was a Protector, but I listened carefully to Jet as he continued.

"He picked up that log all by himself and threw it clear onto the bank!!" Jet's eyes were wide open.

I looked over at the huge log that had trapped the wild pig just moments ago. "That's not possible, that log must weigh at least half a ton, no fairy is that strong. Are you sure the water didn't shift it like he said it did?"

"LOLA, I know what I saw. It was quick I'll grant you that, but he definitely lifted it and threw it away, I'm positive!" Jet replied.

"The plot thickens," I said mostly to myself.

What teacher needs the strength of ten fairies? And if he's not a teacher and is indeed a Protector, why is he here in the Blue Mountains and why is he pretending to be a teacher? More importantly, why is the Headmaster keeping his real purpose a secret? I wondered.

"I'm now 100% convinced that you are right, LOLA. Something is going on and we need to find out what it is before it's too late," replied Jet with a steely look of determination in his eyes.

HOPING FOR A MIRACLE

I awoke before dawn, after another night of tossing and turning. I was anxious to meet with Allie and Jet and go over the events of the night before. I hadn't seen much of Allie at the dance, so I was curious to find out what she overheard. Jet and I were also still wondering about the super fairy efforts of one mysterious Mr. Thomas Holt.

We had agreed to meet in the field out behind the school; it was pretty quiet there on Sundays, so we knew we were unlikely to be disturbed. Jet was already there when I arrived, so we sat in thoughtful silence and waited for Allie to join us. When she finally arrived, all flustered and apologizing for being late, I decided to cut right to the chase.

"Allie, Jet and I have a fair bit to tell you, but why don't you go first? We hardly saw you all night, what did you find out?" I asked.

"Well actually, I had a very interesting conversation with a lovely fairy called Jess. Did you happen to see our new teacher dancing with a very beautiful stranger?" asked Allie.

"Yes, as a matter of fact I was wondering who that was," I replied.

"Well, it turns out that she *loved* my dress and when she found out that I made it myself, she begged me to make her a whole new wardrobe." Allie was full of excitement. I was starting to wonder where this was going. I hoped she hadn't just been talking about dresses all night!

"Apparently Jess is an old and very close friend of Mr. Holt and she is currently trying to woo him. She went to school with him right here in the Blue Mountains and had hoped to marry him, but he disappeared in suspicious circumstances right after they graduated and she's never heard from him since... that was nearly ten years ago and she'd assumed he was dead. She'd almost forgotten about him, until last week when she was here visiting her mother and just happened to bump into him in broad daylight. She almost fainted, what with assuming him dead and all."

"Get to the point Allie!" urged Jet, losing the will to live.

"My point is, Mr. Impatient Pants, that she claims she was SO surprised to find out that he was a teacher now, because she was sure he'd gone off to some extreme place to become a warrior or something. That's all he ever talked about at school, and when he disappeared and didn't come back, she assumed he'd succeeded and died in some kind of battle. How's that for a theory? She reckons he was the strongest fairy in the school and the fact that he's become a teacher is *totally unexpected* - her words, I swear!" Allie was hoping this would help; she wasn't usually much good at this spy stuff and desperately wanted to help her friends.

"This completely backs up what I saw LOLA, I knew it!" shouted Jet.

Jet proceeded to fill Allie in on what he had witnessed the night before, that being the super strength of Mr. Holt lifting and throwing the massive log off the young pig. Allie's huge eyes widened even further as she listened on in awe.

"Okay let's examine the facts, we need a list so that we don't get carried away and miss something important." I had paper and pen at the ready of course, everyone knows that there's nothing I like more than a good list!

What We Know so Far:

1. There was a terrible disaster in 1985 where most of the fairy community of the Blue Mountains was killed or captured - *not too sure yet why it happened but we know that humans were to blame.*

2. The entire history of 1985 has been wiped from all record – *implying the King, the school and everyone in power must be in on the cover up.*

3. The new teacher (now revealed to be Mr. Thomas Holt) is posing as a teacher, but is definitely not what he seems – *he*

has amazing strength equal to at least ten fairies – we suspect he might be a Protector Fairy.

4. Mrs. Macc left her post under suspicious circumstances so that Mr. Holt could take her place in the school – *does she know something?*

5. Thomas Holt has warned the Headmaster of some imminent threat to the community, but the Headmaster is not sharing this news with anyone – *he seems scared of the King finding out. Why?*

"Okay, so I think we are all agreed. Something is very wrong," I stated. After seeing the facts in black and white, I was now absolutely certain of this fact.

"Mr. Holt must be here to protect us from something, but what? And why is the Headmaster not raising the alarm? Surely if the school and the whole fairy community is under any kind of threat, he has to tell the King and Queen or at the very least our parents!" I reasoned.

Jet and Allie just nodded, the truth was that none of us really knew what was going on or what to do about it.

"I don't see any other option, we have to take this to the highest powers, we have to tell the King and Queen. We'll tell them what I overheard and all the suspicious things we have learned and they will fix it!" I was certain that this was the right thing to do. I suspected that we might be in a *bit* of trouble for eavesdropping on the Headmaster and for sticking our noses in, BUT surely they would be outraged when they knew that there was a potential threat to our community and they hadn't been told!

"I hate to admit it, but I think you're right LOLA. This is bigger than us and as we don't know what the threat is or when it's coming, we've hit a dead end," replied Jet matter-of-factly.

"But how are we going to get in front of the King and Queen?" asked Allie quite rightly. Everyone knows that normal fairies can't get an audience with royalty that easily; they're far too busy!

"Allie, what about if you offer your services as dressmaker to the Princess? Her wedding is coming up soon and they haven't announced who will be making her dress yet. All we need to do is get the Princess to see your designs and want YOU to make her dress." It was a long shot, but it was the best I could come up with.

Allie did not look convinced.

"LOLA, there's no way I'm experienced enough for that. Yes I make dresses for you and my friends and the odd paying customer, but I'm nowhere near talented enough for the Princess to let me make her wedding dress!"

"I have to agree with Allie," added Jet. "No offense Allie, you're dead talented and all that, but there are much more experienced dressmakers in this town and how are we supposed to get the Princess to see Allie's dresses anyway?"

He had a point, but I wasn't giving up that easily. We just had to get in front of the King and Queen and I could think of no other option.

We decided to sleep on it. I could tell that Jet and Allie thought it was a lost cause, but experience had taught me that sometimes all that was needed was a good night's sleep and your mind would do the rest. Here's hoping for a miracle, I thought...

NINE

ALLIE TO THE RESCUE

It was another beautiful day in the Blue Mountains. As I woke and stared out of my skylight, I could see the sun hitting the tops of the trees and the forest was buzzing with all kinds of birds, butterflies, bees and wasps doing their early morning swoops around the mountains.

I decided to join them, there was nothing like an early morning flight to clear the mind and wake up the body. I swooped through the trees, riding the currents of the wind and getting a nice speed on the way down into the valleys. Swallows joined me playfully as I soared through the valley and skimmed across gushing waterfalls. I laughed as I flew, dreaming of one day flying further afield, exploring other countries even and seeing sights I had never seen before. I knew it was only a dream as the King would never allow it, but I let myself get carried away in the pure pleasure of my imagination.

Coming back down to earth, I let the events of the past few days turn over in my head. Sleep had done little to change my mind; in fact I was now certain. Our *only* option was to somehow get the attention of the Princess and make her WANT Allie to make her dress. I believed in Allie's dressmaking skills, even if she didn't, and I knew that with a little help, this was a plan that just might work!

Jet and Allie were easy to find, they'd been for an early fly together and I spotted them landing as I approached Allie's house.

"So I've been thinking about what I suggested last night and I'm certain that it's the best plan we have," I told them confidently.

"We've been thinking too and... we agree, but I can't do it alone," replied Allie. Frankly I was stunned, I expected I'd have to win them over but now they were both agreeing with me.

"I found out from my Mum that the Princess has announced a competition," Allie continued quite excitedly. "Apparently, it was announced last night and hasn't hit the grapevine yet, but the prize is that the winning dressmaker gets to make the dress for not only the Princess but also the Queen herself! This could really launch me professionally speaking, something like this might even convince my Mum to let me set up a little shop on the side!"

I was doubtful that Allie's Mum would be keen for her to start her career whilst she was still at school, but I was happy that Allie was so excited.

"That's great Allie, but don't forget what the REAL mission is here, and that's to get in front of the King and Queen!" I reminded her.

"We need to make sure Allie wins first though," replied Jet quite rightly.

"I better get to work then, The deadline is next Sunday, so I have less than a week to make the best dress of my life. Plus, we still have to go to school, so I'll have to work every night to even have a hope of finishing it in time!" said Allie in a fluster.

"Don't worry Allie, we'll help. Tell us, what we can do?" I asked.

"Well I'll need materials, lots of them. I'll start my drawings today and when I know what fabrics and dyes I need, if you and Jet can collect them for me that will be a big help. Half the work is in the set up. If I can focus on the designs whilst you hunt and gather, that will cut my time in half. Then I'll need a model. LOLA, that will have to be you. As the dress starts to take shape, I'll need someone to try it on and move around in it so I can make sure it's comfortable and looks nice whilst it moves."

Allie continued to list off all the things she'd need, Jet volunteered to help her with homework so she didn't fall behind at school (and more importantly get in trouble with her parents), and we both agreed to keep a sneaky eye on the competition. Every dressmaker (amateur or professional) in the Blue Mountains would be dying to win this prize, so we had to be one step ahead of them.

Allie got straight to work at her drawing desk. Jet and I killed time by play fighting in her yard and we told her to yell when she had some instructions for us. It wasn't too long before Allie shouted us in. We zipped inside, quick as a flash, and asked to see her drawings.

"Oh no, not yet. I'm still sketching out ideas, but I do know some of the materials I need to get me started."

Allie listed off what to us sounded like a *bizarre* list of materials, but we wrote them down as instructed, and went off in search of everything.

Allie's List of Materials:

Thinly striped bark from a eucalyptus tree
Fern leaves
Silk worms (as many as we could persuade to join us!)
Bright pink hydrangeas
Wild cherries
Wild blackberries
Stinging nettles
Pinecones
Spikes from echidnas
Feathers fallen from birds in flight
Honeycomb from the bees

I think you'll agree it takes a LOT of imagination to see how these things could possibly be used to make a dress, but confident in Allie's creative genius, we went off in search of all the items on the list. Jet and I decided to split up to have a better chance of success. Some of the items would be hard to find. We split the list up between us equally and wished each other good luck.

As the light from the sun faded, I made my way back to Allie's house, dragging behind me a net filled with weird and wonderful things. I was hoping she'd be pleased with my loot as it was very hard to convince 20 silk worms to join our cause, but I promised them praise from the whole town if we were successful. I also had to promise them a never-ending supply of Mulberry leaves (this is all silk worms eat and it is very hard to find), and they finally agreed to come with me and produce as much silk as Allie needed to make her dress.

Jet arrived shortly afterwards with an equally overflowing bag of goodies. We gave them all to Allie, still not quite sure what she had planned. She quietly thanked us and promised that it would all make sense soon. She would still need other odds and ends, but they could come later. For now she had enough to finish her designs, and she felt confident that she had the materials she needed to get started tomorrow.

We took the hint, Allie was asking us to leave her be so that she could concentrate on her work without being interrupted. Exhausted from our day of hunting and gathering, Jet and I were only too happy to go home and get some well-deserved rest. It was going to be a busy week.

The next week flashed by in a blur of schoolwork and fetching things for Allie. Her dressmaking had taken on a frenzied pace as the competition deadline approached, and each day she told us that she'd never be finished in time. But when Sunday arrived, Allie was indeed finished and she invited us over to see the final dress before we went to the Palace to present it to the Princess.

Allie had never asked me to model it; she had decided that she wanted it to be a surprise for everyone, including me, so we hadn't actually seen the dress at all. We arrived early at Allie's house, both eager and slightly nervous to see the dress. We had faith in her of course, but her secrecy had been driving us mad. We sat down, as instructed, whilst Allie went into the dressing room to change.

64

When she finally appeared, we both gasped. She looked STUNNING, like an angel. Somehow, she'd taken all the mysterious materials - barks, fruits, flowers and meters of hand made silk - and turned them into the most spectacular dress we had ever seen. The bodice was covered in what looked like handmade silk flowers, her headdress was a mix of shocking pinks and purple flowers entwined with a crown of vines and wild berries, and the fabric of the dress was falling beautifully over a bell-like structure that bounced in the breeze. The final touch was a pair of finely threaded glitter wings that seemed to dance in the sunlight. She was a vision.

We were dumbstruck and Allie basked in the attention, twirling this way then that and fluttering her wings.

"Allie you've done it!" I cried.

"Yes Allie, you've really outdone yourself. You're bound to win!" agreed Jet.

"Do you really think so?" asked Allie, smiling broadly.

"Absolutely, I've been keeping an eye on the competition, and I haven't seen anything as beautiful as this," I replied.

The moment had arrived. I was now certain that thanks to Allie, we would definitely meet the Princess and that meant we'd also meet the King and Queen. A bolt of nerves ran through me and I had a quick flash of fear. I shook it off, as there was no place for nerves today. It was my destiny to alert the King and save the town, I was sure of it.

AN AUDIENCE WITH THE
KING AND QUEEN

The Royal Grounds sparkled like diamonds, the sun was high and bright and it reflected off the Palace windows in beams of silver and gold. We'd never been inside the Royal Grounds before, so we took a few moments to soak it all in. We entered the huge gates as quietly as church mice, hardly daring to breathe. At the final barrier a Royal guard asked for our passes and ushered us through.

"The competition will be held in the Grand Ballroom and you are to wait in the gardens until your name is called." He pointed us to a fountain in the middle of a beautiful garden full of all manner of flowers and perfectly shaped hedges. All the contestants seemed to share our nerves as we fidgeted whilst waiting to be called. We watched as fairy after fairy disappeared behind huge wooden doors with big brass knuckles.

Finally it was our turn.

"Number 26, please follow me," a stern fairy beckoned us to follow her.

"This is it guys. Remember Allie, you'll show the Princess the dress first, and we want you to win of course, BUT we need to remember why we're here," I whispered.

"Got it LOLA, you jump in as soon as I've showed the Princess the dress," replied Allie nervously.

The stern fairy hurried us towards the front of the room where we could see the King and Queen on their thrones and the Princess sitting primly by the side of the Queen.

"Ah and who do we have now?" the Queen asked the stern fairy.

"Number 26 your Majesty, no formal training I'm afraid," replied the stern fairy quite stiffly.

"And I see that you brought your friends along?" the Queen added with a sneer.

"Yes your Majesty, I brought my friends for moral support," replied Allie.

"Well let's see what you have for us then, shall we?"

The Queen turned to whisper something to the Princess as Allie fumbled to free the dress from its huge bag. As the dress emerged, the expressions on the faces of the Queen and the Princess were priceless. They had clearly underestimated Allie and were both quite stunned by what they saw, their mouths forming into a perfect O and their eyes popping out of their heads.

"Well, well, well!" exclaimed the Queen, actually rising out of her throne to get a closer look.

"Magnificent work young lady, and you have no formal training, is that true?"

"Yes your Majesty, I learned the basics from my Mum and have been making dresses for my friends and for my own pleasure," replied Allie sheepishly.

"I must have this exact dress!" piped up the Princess. "You must show it to no one and you will meet with me to make sure it fits me perfectly. I will accept no other dress, Mother."

"Calm down please, we haven't seen all the dresses yet, it wouldn't be fair to judge without seeing them all," said the Queen.

"I don't care, don't you want me to look beautiful on my wedding day? This is the dress, and I MUST have it!" The Princess stomped her feet, quite forgetting her age and her Royal manners.

I jumped in, sensing that now was my chance!

"Whilst we are here your Majesties, we have something incredibly important and potentially life threatening to tell you!" I shouted in my haste to get the words out.

"Well it hardly seems appropriate, but go ahead if you must," sighed the Queen.

"It has come to our attention, that there is an imminent threat to our town, perhaps even life threatening, and furthermore the Headmaster of the school is aware and does not seem to have brought this matter to your attention. As our ruler, we thought you'd want to know so that you can investigate and organize an evacuation plan if necessary."

The King, Queen and Princess were all shocked by my outburst.

"Silence, what lies are these?" boomed the King.

"They are not lies, your Majesty. We have discovered that there was an attack on the Blue Mountains in 1985 that nearly wiped out the whole community and we think it's going to happen again. We need to increase security and evacuate the whole community whilst there's still time! You were the King in 1985, surely you of all people remember what happened and will stop it from happening again!" I cried.

"How dare you insult the King!" he bellowed. "I am aware of everything in this town. Everything that has ever been or will ever be is under my control, and I can assure you that this great town is completely safe and its security is none of your concern!" he boomed.

"But your Majesty, that is not what we have heard. There's a new teacher at our school and I overheard him talking to the Headmaster, and it sounded like he knew something bad was going to happen. I don't know how he knows this, but you need to do something or we will all die!"

I was getting mad now. Why wasn't he taking this seriously? This was not going how I'd hoped it would, not at all.

"You are dismissed, you will not breathe a word of your lies to anyone else. I'll be having a discussion with your parents and they will decide what to do with you. As for this so-called new teacher, the Headmaster will be hearing from me about this. I decide who teaches in my town. You need to learn to respect authority, young lady. I am the King and if I say there is NO threat, there is NO threat!! I provide safety and security to all who live here and if they abide by my rules, no harm will come to them. That is my final word, now leave and don't think for one minute that my daughter will get married in that dress!"

The Princess moaned and gave me a deathly stare. She was obviously very taken with the dress and now my little speech had ruined it all.

We left the room in stunned disgrace.

Allie was crying softly and Jet's face was set as hard as stone. We were too shocked to utter a word to each other until we'd left the Royal Grounds far behind us.

"I don't understand," I turned to face Jet and Allie. "Why was he so angry and so unwilling to listen to a word I said? He is either in complete denial or he's covering something up."

"I think that's the point, LOLA. Think about it, who has the power to wipe an entire year from the records, and who is the highest authority in the land?"

"So you think the King is behind this after all? Maybe the Headmaster was right to keep the new teacher a secret." I thought out loud. It was starting to make a little more sense.

"Exactly! All those rules he has about not travelling, all the new laws he put in place that he said were for our own good. All the bans on reading anything not sanctioned by the King. I bet it's all rubbish. He's just trying to keep us here and under his control!!" Jet was fired up and I knew, I just knew that he was right.

Since I was little, all I could remember were stupid rules. You can't do that, LOLA, or you'll be locked up. You can't say that, LOLA, someone might hear you. Why can't you just accept things the way they are, LOLA? Well I was fed up of rules. I was not going to live under a dictator and clearly our King DID NOT have our best interests at heart. Instead, he had his own, power and control!

Allie hadn't said a word. In our anger, Jet and I hadn't noticed that she was softly weeping, her face all blotchy and red.

"Oh Allie, I'm so sorry. We completely forgot about your dress and how much work you put into it. I'm sorry we ruined it for you," I was deeply sorry for my friend despite my anger at the King.

71

"It's not your fault, I shouldn't have gotten my hopes up. I'm not strong like you guys. I don't have any grand plans to travel the world or be a warrior like you. All I really wanted was to win that competition and start a nice little dressmaking business, and now it's all gone." She was utterly miserable.

"Don't say that Allie, you'll totally be a dressmaker, I'm certain of it. But you know that we had to do what we did, don't you?" I asked her.

"Of course I do. I know that was the real reason we were doing it in the first place, but I can't help it. I got carried away, imagining the Princess in MY dress, and everyone saying how lovely she looked. It was a dream, I know, but I was so close!" implored Allie.

"You heard the Princess, it was her favourite dress by far, no one can take that away from you, Allie. You never know, maybe when the King calms down he will change his mind."

"Fat chance," sighed Allie.

"I hate to be insensitive Allie but we have bigger issues to face. The King is clearly not going to admit that there is a threat to the town, so it's up to us to do something about it AND worse than that, we have to face our parents. I don't know about you guys, but mine are going to flip their lids. To be thrown out of the Royal Grounds for disrespecting the King is not going to go down too well, I imagine," said Jet.

"And then there's school. How will we face the Headmaster now? When he finds out that the King knows about Mr. Holt, we'll be in even more trouble," I added.

This was not good. How long would it take before the King spoke to our parents, I wondered. Dad was going to kill me!
I got home and went straight to my room. I would try to avoid my parents and hope that the King changed his mind and didn't tell them or the Headmaster about today.

No such luck.

Just before dinner, I heard an almighty roar from downstairs.

"LOLA get down here right, now!" Here we go...

"How dare you insult the King? What were you thinking?" bellowed my Dad. "Isn't it enough that I have to go into your school every other week and hear about you disrupting class or being cheeky to your teachers. Now you've made the King mad too!!"

"But Dad..." I tried to tell him MY side of the story.

"But nothing, LOLA, I've heard it all before. You are incapable of doing what you're told. Your head is off in cloud cuckoo land thinking you can travel the world and save everyone in it! It is not your place. You are supposed to go to school, listen and obey your teachers, and try to learn something! Why is that so hard to grasp?" his face had turned a nasty shade of purple and I thought he might explode.

This was so unfair, this was *different* to all the other times, I wanted to cry. But I didn't get the chance.

"Go to your room and don't come down until I tell you to, I do not want to see your face again today. You have disgraced this family. You are GROUNDED for a whole month!"

I turned to look pleadingly at my Mum with tears in my eyes, surely she'd listen to me, surely she'd let me explain....

"I am so disappointed in you, LOLA. Now do as your Father says," was all my Mum said.

Why oh why do I always make such a mess of things? Why can't I just follow the rules, it would be so much easier. I can't help who I am though, can I? I was born this way. I'm not a bad person. I love my friends and (despite being grounded) I also love my parents. I have a destiny bigger than this town, but that's not allowed apparently.

If it's so wrong, why have I always dreamed of it? Why does it feel so real? I don't want to be a boring teacher or a nurse or something (according to them, that's all I'm destined to be!)

Then a thought hit me. I would run away.

I bet no one would even miss me (other than Jet and Allie, and I was sure they'd totally understand). There was nothing left for me in this town and I sure wasn't going to stick around and watch disaster happen, and then what, say I told you so?

I knew one thing for certain. If I didn't leave now, school would be a nightmare, the Headmaster would probably get sacked, Mr. Holt would magically disappear and any hope we had of being saved would be long gone. I was scared and nervous but I had made my decision, I would leave at first light.

ELEVEN

NEW BEGINNINGS

I left before the sun rose. The house was eerily quiet, so I was careful not to make a sound. I packed an extra set of clothing in my backpack and nothing more. I reasoned that I could eat what nature provided and drink from the waterfalls and rivers that I came across.

As I flew through the trees and valleys, and I slowly relaxed and gained in confidence, I allowed myself one final glance at my home in the Blue Mountains as it disappeared into the distance. I promised myself to never look back again.

This was the beginning of my story; this was the birth of LOLA intrepid explorer! I had no idea where I was heading, all I had to guide me was my intuition.

I must have flown for hours and hours before I started to get tired. My head had been working overtime, so I hadn't even noticed what direction I was flying in. I was following my instinct and the strong currents of the wind. I landed on a moss-covered rock in a shaded forest and decided to rest for a little while.

The forest was so quiet in the dead of night. It felt like the world had stopped just for me. I could hear the low rustle of the wind through the trees, and the tiny humming of birds and insects at rest. As I settled into a small nook I found in the rocks, I allowed my mind to roam free. I hoped that Allie and Jet did not get into too much trouble. I felt bad giving them no warning of what I was planning to do, but I knew if I told them that they'd follow me and I couldn't risk getting them into even more trouble. I needed to do this alone.

In the morning after I'd bathed, eaten and drunk my fill of cold clean water from the waterfall, I felt fully rested and ready to set off again. The forest was waking up and the trees were alive with the beautiful sound of birdcall and scampering animals. I took in the sounds of the forest as a plan began to form in my mind.

I remembered a story the caretaker had told me about a community of Water Fairies that lived along the coast in Byron Bay. I decided to make that my first stop. If his stories were true, there were other communities of fairy folk and maybe my destiny lied with them? If he was telling tales, I'd still get to see the sea and I'd never seen the sea, so how bad could it be?

I had never left the Blue Mountains before, for fear of some terrible fate befalling me, or worse still, being arrested and locked up in jail by the King. So my navigation skills were not the best. It was something I would have to improve, and quickly! I decided to ask the birds for help, as surely there are no better navigators of the skies than the birds. There was a nest ahead of me with three swallows, so I called up to them shyly.

"Hi there, I was wondering could you help me please?" I asked.

"Well hello there little one, what can we do to help, are you lost?" the proud mamma swallow replied.

"Yes, I need to get to Byron Bay. I have family there and they are expecting me, but I don't know the way," I decided to bend the truth a little, just in case anyone came looking for me.

"Well you're in luck, you're not far away at all. We're about to take our youngest here off on a training flight, and we can take you most of the way if you like. Do you think you can keep up?" she teased.

"I love a challenge, count me in!" I answered her confidently.

And we were off. I've been on some awesome flights with Jet before, but this went above and beyond anything I'd ever done. Swallows fly like no other birds, they are fast and quick to change direction, and they swoop up and down hills and valleys so effortlessly that it's like they are riding the wind. I was keeping up for most of the journey, but as they swooped into the big valleys, I came unstuck. I had to flap my wings twice as furiously to match their speeds at this height and I was trailing behind. Luckily the mamma swallow saw my struggle and waited for me as I furiously buzzed towards her.

"Hold on to my wing," she shouted above the howls of the wind.

I grasped hold of her wing tightly and held on to her for dear life as she swooped down almost headfirst beside the cliff face. I was laughing for joy as she skimmed across the sea, seeming to float just above it on a current of air. Her wings were hardly moving, it was the most beautiful flight of my life and I didn't want it to end. I clung tightly and watched as the strong waves rolled below us. In the distance I could see the curve of the shoreline as the tide rolled onto sandy beaches. I'd never seen the sea before, oh I'd heard tales, but nothing prepared me for the sight before me - the swirling deep blue waters and frothy tips of the waves were hypnotic and the sandy beaches sparkled along the coastline. It was quite a sight and I hoped beyond all hope that this was our destination.

As if she could hear my thoughts, the mamma swallow answered me.

"There you go, that's Byron Bay right ahead of you. Where does your family live?" she asked.

"Oh they move around a lot, don't worry I'll find them," I said, hoping to avoid any questions that might reveal my little lie.

"I can go alone from here. I'd like to explore a little bit before I see them anyway. Thanks so much for your help, it really was a wonderful ride! What's your name by the way? I'm so sorry I didn't introduce myself earlier, my name is LOLA."

"Why of course, how rude of us. I am Tilda and the quiet one over there is Marty, and the little one is Misty," she replied.

"Well it really was very kind of you to help me, I won't forget it. Hopefully we'll meet again someday and I can return the favour," I added gratefully.

"Your kind do enough for us, don't you worry about that. Just think of us and we'll be there if you need us. Bye now!" replied Tilda as they swooped off into the distance.

What a strange comment I thought, I wonder what she meant by it? I didn't linger on it though, I was so excited by the sight of the sandy beaches in front of me. I wanted to explore. I wasn't exactly sure where to look for Water Fairies as the caretaker hadn't been specific, but I assumed that by the sea was a good place to start! I flew slowly down the length of the coast, taking in the spectacular scenery and breathing the fresh salty air.

Set back from the coast were hundreds of beautiful buildings in a range of pastel colours, they were obviously human houses. I had never been this close to so many humans before and the noise of them swimming in the sea and playing on the beaches was quite startling. I have to admit I was a bit frightened, but I pushed the fearful thoughts away, they would do me no good. It was hard to stay focused with so many distractions, but I was determined to find some sign of fairy life so I slowly made my way up the beaches, skimming the waves and enjoying the spray of fresh salty water as it hit my face.

I had almost given up hope, when out of the corner of my eye I saw a couple of bright lights chasing each other across the sea. I stopped in my tracks and stared intently at where I thought I'd seen the lights. The waves were playful and light reflected off them like diamonds, so it was hard to tell if what I was seeing was underneath the surface or just reflections from the sun.

Then something zipped out of the water and nearly bowled me clean over. It was a fairy, closely followed by another one! I couldn't believe it, the caretaker was telling the truth, and Water Fairies did exist!

I sat back stunned and delighted and watched them darting across the water, skimming their heels and buzzing playfully. It looked like such fun, so I didn't have the heart to interrupt them. I took the chance to get a good look at them. They certainly looked a lot like me, their bodies were longer and their wings seemed thinner and longer too, but you could definitely see the resemblance. They were electric green in colour, with huge blue eyes and long legs and they moved at lightning speed. I think they'd even give Jet a good race.

I wondered, did they live under the sea or just near it? I had so many questions tumbling through my mind that I hadn't noticed that they had stopped chasing each other and were now checking me out.

"You're not from around here are you?" asked the larger of the two.

"Yeah, I've never seen you before, where are you from?" added the smaller one.

I realized that in my haste to leave, I hadn't really gotten my story straight, which was unusual for me. I would have to trust my instincts. Right now I didn't feel threatened, these fairies looked young and harmless enough, so I decided to be honest with them.

"I've left my home in search of somewhere better," I answered, which was true enough without giving too much away. "I don't know what my future holds, but I knew I was in danger where I was, so I left," I added.

"Danger? But you're a fairy, how can you be in any danger?" they asked.

"It's a long story," I told them. "The town I'm from was once almost wiped out by humans and it's going to happen again. There's nothing I can do to stop it and no one believed me when I tried to warn them, so I left." I added in a defeated tone. Until this moment I hadn't realized just how much my failure to get through to the King and my parents had upset me. I felt utterly miserable.

They exchanged glances that told me they clearly thought I was quite mad.

"Come with us, I think there's someone you should meet. My name is Paige and this is my sister, Eva. You need to meet our Queen, she'll be able to help you, I'm sure of it," Paige told me confidently and before I could answer, she sped off across the water with Eva following close behind.

Without thinking, I followed in hot pursuit, curious to meet their Queen and yet slightly fearful of what I might find. My brushes with Royalty had not ended well so far!

We came to rest in a deserted cove. Nestled into the shoreline it was a peaceful spot, away from the humans having fun in the sea, and I could see no sign of life.

"Follow us," Paige called to me over her shoulder as she slipped into a tiny opening in the curve of the rocks.

I followed tentatively, not sure where they were leading me and quite unprepared for the sights that lay ahead. As my eyes adjusted, I could see tiny pathways all lit up by some type of fluorescent plant. It looked like a maze, almost a complete copy of our underground homes, but cool and fresh with the calming sounds of sea water trickling down the rock walls. We stopped in a large room with what looked like a hundred rows of tiny houses on each side, all looking directly onto the main cave. I quickly surveyed the room and could see hundreds of fairies all going about their business in their homes and at least fifty more flitting and buzzing in and out of the tunnels. No one seemed to be particularly interested in me, so I stood quietly and waited for my new friends to take me to their Queen.

I didn't have to wait long. Paige flitted up another passageway and came back with a huge grin on her face followed by a Water Fairy of such grace and beauty that I had to pinch myself to make sure I wasn't dreaming. This was obviously their Queen.

Her hair was a magnificent snakes nest of colour, made up of orange, green and yellow glimmering spirals that trailed far behind her. Her body was lean and well muscled, indicating a strength that matched her beauty. She was tall and grand with a peaceful kind face, and it is safe to say that I loved her on first sight.

"We are so thrilled to have you visit us, my young one. May we know the reason for this unexpected visit?" Her voice was like silk, and listening to her talk felt like slipping into a warm bath of honey. Something about her gaze had my words spilling from my mouth before I could even think them. I was like a tap and once turned on there was no stopping me.

"My name is LOLA and I have travelled a long way to meet others of my kind. The town I come from is under threat from humans, but our King is in denial and when I tried to warn him of the threat, he got very angry and threw me out of the Palace. My parents were told that I had insulted the King and they said I had disgraced them, so I ran away. We were always told that if we ever left the Blue Mountains, we would be captured and killed by humans and that the world isn't safe for fairies. But here I am, and so far I haven't been captured or killed, so I think the King has been lying to us!"

The Queen nodded and paused, with the same calm look on her face. So far she hadn't shouted or called me rude, so I felt safe enough to keep talking.

"It's my destiny to save the town, I know it is, but I don't know what to do. How will I make anyone take me seriously if the King has publicly disgraced me, and what if it's already too late?" I realized as the words tumbled out of my mouth that my biggest fear was that I had abandoned my family and friends to suffer a terrible fate and that I would be powerless to stop it. The thought brought fresh tears to my eyes and pain to my heart. I hastily wiped my tears away and tried to be strong in front of the Queen.

"LOLA, I will try to answer your questions and your fears one by one, as there are many," she paused to collect her thoughts. "Firstly, my name is Katia and I am the Queen of the Water Fairies. I provide sanctuary, purpose and community for my tribe and yet I am not their master. Fairy folk do not need masters, this is one of the first lessons I will teach you as it seems that you have not been educated in the true ways of our kind."

She smiled with her eyes and patted the ground next to her to indicate that I should sit comfortably and listen.

"Secondly I have heard of your King and I'm afraid your instincts are indeed correct. He has suffered terrible losses over the years and as a result he has become scared and closed-minded. He rules his Kingdom with fear and by shunning the rest of the fairy community. He is weak and scared of change, and I'm afraid all too often weak men use fear to hold on to their remaining power and influence. He cannot admit that he made any mistakes in the past or that he is no longer capable of leading his people. So he rules with fear and from the sounds of it, successfully so..." she mused.

"But you, LOLA, you give me hope. Your spirit was not quashed! You KNEW there was more to life and you came out looking for it and you found us! You don't realize it yet, but there is great power within you LOLA, I can sense it. There IS a destiny unfolding for you as we speak and you can count on us to help you find it!"

"Wow," was all I managed to splutter out, I was stunned and deliriously happy all at once. This meant that I WAS NOT mad, this meant all those times I'd known that there was more to life, I was right! And could I dare to believe that there was hope for my friends and family after all, and that the Queen of the Water Fairies would help me save them?
Oh it was all just *too* good to be true. Just one day ago I'd almost given up hope, and now I had a whole new life ahead of me!

"Paige and Eva, you brought LOLA to us, so I will give you both the honour of educating her in our magical ways. If I know anything about her King - and believe me I do - she won't know half of the things she's capable of and you will have to teach her. Start with the basics - glimmering, fairy dust, mindreading, protective shields and communicating with animals. Then when she has mastered those, we can get into the more serious stuff—invisibility, stopping time, affecting the weather and finally communicating with humans as spirit guides..."

WHAT!! My brain was in shock and denial...

"Err can you repeat some of those please, I lost you at mindreading... I think you might have the wrong end of the stick. I'm not like you, I'm a Mountain Fairy and we obviously don't have the powers and skills that you have."

"Nonsense, every fairy is born with the same powers," insisted the Queen. "You have just never been taught how to use them, it's very simple really. Your King wanted to keep you as loyal followers, never questioning his rule and never leaving the Kingdom. So the easiest way to do that was by not teaching you to develop the very skills that you were born with. It's outrageous I know, but I'm afraid it's true. After the terrible events that happened in 1985, of which I am sadly very much aware, your King decided to enforce strict laws from birth.

"You see, he was convinced that if fairies did not use their magical powers, then there would be no reason for humans to want to capture us and experiment on us. So he made it illegal for any fairy to use any magical powers that would draw attention. The basics such as flight, glimmering and the odd bit of fairy dust were allowed, as these were all skills that go unnoticed. But anything outside of that was outlawed at home and at school. And gradually as time moved on, fairies living in his Kingdom forgot they even had such powers and accepted the King's rules. The final nail in the coffin was banning all travel out of the Kingdom, that way he could be sure you wouldn't meet other fairies like us and would never learn of your true powers."

I listened on intently, I was so glad to finally know the truth that I forgot about how angry I was with the King. I was just excited to learn about my *true* powers and ready to try them out.

"The rest of the fairy world have embraced change. We have enhanced our skills, we teach our young to develop their full potential from birth and as a result we are in perfect harmony with ourselves and the world around us. There is nothing we fear and by the time I'm finished with you, young LOLA, there will be nothing you fear either," she added with a wide grin.

I was just about to launch into a thousand questions when she made it clear that this was the end of our little chat.

"No more words today, LOLA. I can see you still have a lot of questions, but there will be time for all that, I promise. I have other business to attend to. I will leave you with Paige and Eva, I am sure you will be great friends and they will help you to settle in. I suggest you get a good night's rest as tomorrow will be a very busy day."

And with those words she was gone. It was hard to pinpoint exactly how I felt. My entire life was based on lies. Apparently I had crazy skills that no one had ever told me about. The small world I had left behind was about to become a BIG world, and although it's all I'd ever dreamed of, part of me never thought it would *actually* happen. So you could say I was angry, excited, scared and jumping for joy all at the same time. One thing was for sure. My life would never be the same again, and I had the beautiful Queen of the Water Fairies to thank.

TWELVE

NEW FRIENDS AND MAD SKILLS

After a surprisingly good night's sleep, I was awoken by the shrill cries and giggles of Paige and Eva, followed in hot pursuit by a little fairy that resembled a bumblebee. He was plump and furry with a dopey grin on his face. I was immediately intrigued by him and promptly introduced.

"LOLA meet Banjo, Banjo this is LOLA," giggled Eva.

"Pleased to meet you miss, you're dressed funny, you've got big boots on," he stared at me with a friendly innocence that made him very likeable.

"I suppose I do look a bit out of place, don't I?" I replied good-humoredly. I knew he meant no offense - my big black work boots, camouflage trench coat and bright blue hair did look a bit out of place in this seaside setting.

"Don't be rude, Banjo. You don't get out much, so certain things seem new and strange to you. You should try travelling further afield from time to time, expand your horizons like the Queen is always telling us to!" snapped Paige, quick to jump to my defense.

"It's okay really, I understand. This is all new to me too. Where I come from we aren't allowed to travel at all, so I've only ever seen fairies that look very much like me. I've certainly never seen a gold and black striped fellow as handsome as you before!" I whispered to Banjo. I'd already decided to like him very much.

This seemed to please Banjo and he accepted my answer and my strange clothing without further question. Paige and Eva had strict instructions that my lessons should begin immediately, so as soon as we had eaten breakfast and done a few high-speed laps of the coastline for exercise, it was down to business.

I'd like to say that my first day went well, but sadly that wasn't the case. I started with glimmering, and whilst I thought I was already pretty good at glimmering, it turns out I had very limited skills. Yes I could change my hair colour and my wings to whatever shade I wanted, but when it came to glimmering my surroundings, I came unstuck.

Like I was told, I concentrated hard on making my surroundings match me. I closed my eyes and imagined a mountain scene from the Blue Mountains, but all I managed to do was turn everyone's hair green! Banjo found this hilarious (imagine a bumblebee with green spiky hair). After five or six bungled attempts, I was getting mad and I had to have a time out to calm down. My teachers were very patient with me at first, but as the morning dragged on, their occasional sighs and furtive glances to each other told me that they were losing patience with my repeated mistakes and outbursts of temper.

After about three hours of frustration and not much success, Paige told Eva and Banjo to go and find us some lunch and take a break. She sat me down on the bank and allowed me to cool down.

"I think LOLA, if you don't mind me saying so, that your problem isn't that you're not trying hard enough, but that you're trying TOO hard..."

I was about to make a smart comment in return, but then I let her words sink in. Could she be right, was I trying too hard?

"Why don't we try again, whilst we are alone and there are no distractions? This time I don't want you to TRY at all, I want you to let go and trust that the answers are inside you and will be available to you when you need them," Paige instructed.

"Okaaaay," I replied. It sounded pointless to me, but it was worth a shot.

"Let's try a different skill this time, like mindreading. I know you can do this, just sit back and close your eyes. Breathe deeply and try to clear your mind. I will say something to you using my mind, and you will try and tell me what I said. Now remember, it doesn't matter if you get it wrong, just trust your instincts and tell me the first thing that comes into your head," instructed Paige.

I closed my eyes and tried to stay calm. I focused on my breathing just like she said, on the breath entering my body and leaving it, and then I waited. I kept my eyes closed for a few minutes and nothing happened, and then a flicker, just a flicker of an image appeared like a picture from a movie. I tried to hold it in my mind. I was nervous telling her what I saw, as I wasn't confident at all. Wasn't I supposed to hear words, not see a picture?

"I didn't hear anything… but I saw an image of a plate of berries. Maybe I'm just hungry?" I hurriedly added, quite sure that I'd failed again.

"No LOLA, that's exactly right! I was thinking about lunch and I was hoping for a big plate of juicy berries. You did it!" she cried, she was so happy that she danced a little jig in the air.

It was hard to not get carried away by doing something right for a change, but something told me that she was just being nice, so I asked her some more questions.

"But why did I see an image and not hear any words?"

"Sorry, that's my fault for not explaining it properly. Some fairies see images and some hear words. There's no right or wrong way to read minds, it's just what works best for you. You must be a visual person, so your brain gave you an image. As you strengthen your skills, most likely you'll start seeing both images and words, BUT as long as you understand the meaning, it doesn't matter. It's a great start LOLA. Let's wait for the others to arrive before we continue. Have some lunch and then you can practice some more."

I sat back and thought about the lessons so far. I'd been so concerned with getting it right and not looking stupid in front of my new friends that I was my own worst enemy. I realized that I was still trying to prove myself, to my family, my friends, the teachers, the King, in fact anyone who had ever doubted me. It was slowly dawning on me that the only person I needed to prove anything to was myself. I promised then and there to give myself a break and not be so hard on myself when I got things wrong.

The afternoon lessons were much more successful and I was soon having a great time. By letting go and trusting my instincts, hours went past without me even noticing. I learned how to create a protective shield around myself; I even managed to build one that encircled all four of us, much to Banjo's delight, as that was his special talent!

I got better and better at controlling my mind and tuning into the thoughts and feelings of the fairies and animals around me - so much so that I had to learn how to turn it off again, as the noise was deafening. I improved my glimmering skills by a crazy amount. Until then, I'd been able to change the colour of my body, clothes, wings and hair, but by the end of the first day, I could successfully change the appearance of my surroundings to completely camouflage myself. It was amazing how much I had learned, and thankfully my teachers seemed much happier with me, which was a relief.

The next week followed the same daily pattern. Paige, Eva and Banjo would wake me up early and take me to a different location to practice. The Queen was happy with my progress and I was cleared to learn the more advanced magic, to say I was excited was an understatement! I decided to keep a journal to track my progress and write notes about anything tricky I had to keep practicing.

LOLA's New Skills:

Mindreading - 7/10 getting better but definitely need more practice.

Glimmering – 9/10 this has improved the most, I can't wait to show Allie my new mad skills!

Protective shields – 8/10 if I concentrate, the shield is really strong, but sometimes my mind wanders off. Must focus LOLA!

Affecting time and weather – 5/10 this is REALLY hard, I need a lot more practice. Paige and Eva said I might be able to

THE ADVENTURES OF LOLA

get personal lessons with the Queen, as she is the best at these powers.

Communicating with animals – 10/10 the Queen says I am now fully trained and all I need to do now is talk to animals as often as possible and learn about their ways, she says this may be useful if I ever need their help.

Invisibility – 8/10 I'm really good at this if I'm in a good mood, when I'm grumpy I still seem to have an outline so I'm not 100% invisible. I'm not sure why that is, I must find out!

Overall, I was pretty happy with my progress. It was amazing how quickly things that seemed really hard on the first day became second nature. My only disappointment was that I hadn't been able to ask the Queen of the Water Fairies the million questions I still had for her. It seemed as if she was deliberately avoiding me. Every time I got back to the caves after hours of training, she would hurry off on some important job or another. In the mornings before we left, she was nowhere to be seen.

Then finally at the end of a very long week, when I was beginning to think that she didn't like me, she came to the dancing tree and found me nestled in the branches. The dancing tree was my favourite spot in Byron Bay; it's where I went to collect my thoughts at the end of each day. I called it the dancing tree as it never quite sat still, it was charmed no doubt. No matter how still the air was, or how calm the sea was, its leaves danced as if in league with some imaginary wind machine. All the trees around it would be perfectly still, and yet the dancing tree would shimmer and sway. I just loved it. I could sit there for hours watching the crashing waves hit the beach and see dolphins jumping out of the sea in the distance.

"How did you know where to find me?" I asked the Queen.

"LOLA, I know you are here every day, and I know that this is your special place. I can't say that I blame you, it really is quite bewitching isn't it?" she smiled.

"It's like the tree has music playing that only it can hear, I find it very peaceful," I replied.

"Who knows why it dances LOLA, that's the beauty of nature, some things are not meant to be understood, just accepted and loved exactly as they are," she replied.

"I was beginning to think you were ignoring me." I said, trying not to sulk.

"Not at all. I was merely giving you the time and the space that you needed to focus on your new skills. I must say you are doing very well, even better than I thought you would," she beamed.

"Well everyone has been incredibly patient with me and although I found it really hard at first, I think I'm finally getting the hang of it."

"So do you think you're ready for the final challenge?" she asked.

"I think so," I stuttered, not sure what she would say next.

"The final challenge is to study humans. If you learn to read their auras, you will learn which humans are magical and which are not."

"What's an aura?" I asked.

"An aura is an energy field that surrounds all living things. In a human, if you learn to see and read their aura, you can tell what type of person they are. Children and some adults operate on a similar wavelength to us and there's a trick to spotting them. Once you can do this, you can use your mindreading and communicating skills to talk to them. I've personally found great joy in some of the friendships I have with both children and adults."

"But what if we get it wrong, isn't that incredibly dangerous?" I was still hearing the words of warning that had been drummed into me since birth. *Humans are dangerous, humans mean us harm and we must avoid them at all cost!*

The Queen laughed softly.

"LOLA, the worst thing that can happen is that it doesn't work. If you choose to communicate with a human and they can't hear you, then nothing bad will happen, they just won't hear you. Don't worry, we will keep a safe distance and remember you can now camouflage yourself into your surroundings if it makes you feel more comfortable. I'll be with you the whole time. No harm will come to you, I promise. Take a chance," she urged. I pushed aside all the nagging fears in my head and decided to trust her, she hadn't steered me wrong so far.

As I followed Katia the Queen of the Water Fairies into the night, I was highly aware of all my senses. I'd never felt so alive. My skin picked up even the slightest gust of wind, my hair felt electrified and I could see more clearly than ever before. I felt more magical than I had in my entire life and I had the Queen and my new friends to thank. By the time we came to a sudden stop on the windowsill of an old wooden house, I felt calm and ready for anything.

"LOLA, I want to you to look inside this window," instructed the Queen.

I peered inside. I could see four humans sitting around a table and a dog at the man's feet. The dog spotted me immediately, and I thought for a minute he would start barking. I told him (in my mind) that we meant him no harm. He snuffled slightly, then lowered his head and closed his eyes. Relieved at the lucky escape, I focused my attention on the four humans.

"Now, what do you see LOLA?" asked the Queen.

"Erm, I see four humans and a dog," I answered, not quite sure what I was supposed to be looking for.

"And can you see anything around each human, different colours radiating from them perhaps? Look closely LOLA, look with your third eye," she urged.

"My third eye?" I had no idea what she was talking about; I only had two eyes!!

"Yes LOLA, to access your third eye, you stare at the object ahead of you and let your eyesight go blurry. Then, you are tuned into the energy fields instead of the object. If you do this for long enough and practice hard enough, you will see colours appear around the object. This is the 'aura' that I told you about earlier... now don't rush it, take your time and let me know when you see it."

I did as I was told and focused on the first human. I picked the woman - she was middle aged and kind looking with a lined smiley face. I let my eyes go blurry. I allowed the size and shape of her to morph and shimmer in front of me. At first all I could see was a blur, then slowly, bit-by-bit I started to see waves of colour coming off her. It was like seeing gas flames on a stove, the colour was pale and hard to get a grasp on, but it was definitely a very fine palette of colours, like a rainbow surrounding her body. I could see mostly pinks and purples with some orange and yellow streaks. I told Katia what I could see and she urged me on encouragingly.

"Very good, now focus on each person one at a time and tell me what you see."

I switched my attention to the little girl sitting to her left, who was now reaching down and stroking the dog as he slept. The colours surrounding her were light blue and silvery white, they were quite beautiful. The man was darker and harder to see, his colours were dimmer, as though the light had been turned down to a very low level - he was a dark shade of blue with small specks of red.

The Queen listened intently as I told her what I'd seen. She didn't say anything, she just smiled a funny little smile.

"So what do the colours mean?" I asked her.

"Each of the colours has a different meaning and most people have a few colours that make up their auras. The colors can change depending on their mood," she replied.

"Let's take the lady, for example. You saw pink, purple, orange and yellow, these are good colours - they mean she is kind, intelligent and loving. The little girl is interesting, I strongly suspect her to be magical. Silver is the colour of psychic ability and openness and I think it would be very easy to communicate with her if you wished. The man is more troubled than the others; the darker colours you saw surrounding him mean he is sad and tired, he probably works too hard."

"So could we communicate with the little girl safely?" I asked. I was quite curious now to try it.

"We could yes, but we won't do that today. This was purely an exercise to connect you with your abilities, and you've done very well I might add! Besides it's always best to talk to children when they are alone, she might be concerned what her parents will think and that will stunt her imagination.

No, what I'd like to do now is to introduce you to a very dear friend of mine; she is an artist living nearby. She is what we call a pure silver spirit. A human with a pure silver spirit is what's known as a psychic or a medium in the human world. She is in perfect balance with nature and the spirit world and has been a friend and protector of fairies since childhood. You will meet her and then you might understand why I say there is no reason to fear humans," she suggested.

I was excited and nervous to meet this human. Before today, I'd never been within 20 feet of a human, let alone actually talk to one. It would be unheard of in the Blue Mountains; the King would have a fit! My nerves jittered slightly, but I felt calm and ready for anything.

The artist's house was located deep in the heart of the Hinterlands high above Byron Bay. The surrounding gardens were teaming with fragrant flowers, butterflies, wasps, bees and small lizards. As we approached, she met us at the front door and upon spotting the Queen, she beamed from ear to ear.

"Reaya, it's so good to see you, the garden's looking wonderful!" exclaimed Katia.

"Katia my dear friend, I had a funny feeling you'd be visiting me today, and that you'd bring me a new friend. This must be her... oh I am so pleased to meet you, LOLA. Katia has told me all about you," Reaya turned to face me and smiled warmly.

As my eyes met with hers, I was astounded by the speed at which her aura appeared. I wasn't even trying to see it, but it was so brilliant that it was all I could see. It was as if her whole face was bathing in a pool of silver light and I was overcome by a feeling of immense joy and understanding. I struggled to find the words to reply.

"Ha ha, that's okay LOLA," laughed the Queen. "I see you've been overwhelmed by the force of Reaya's aura, it is quite something isn't it!"

"Well yes, it's nothing like at the house with the other humans. I didn't even have to try and see it, it is just there," I answered still completely bewildered by the dazzling sight.

"Ah, that's why I brought you here LOLA," replied the Queen.

"There are thousands of humans all over the globe who have the gift, and I want you to be able to spot them easily. As I told you, Reaya has been a friend of mine since she was a child. She was born with this gift, and she is in perfect harmony with nature and all magical life. It is a rare gift and some children lose it as they get older, but some special humans keep the gift for life. These are people we seek out, because they protect us from danger, they alert us to threats and they can help us make the world a better place."

"Well I'm honoured to meet you Reaya," I managed.

"And I you, LOLA. I expect great things from you my young friend, I see a pure spirit, full of hope and courage," she smiled again with her eyes and I felt a peace settle over me once more.

After Katia and Reaya had discussed the latest goings on in their worlds and I'd been shown some of Reaya's artwork, we said our goodbyes and flew back to the cave in peaceful silence. My mind was churning, making sense of all I'd learnt. It seemed like five minutes ago that I was forced to leave my home in disgrace and now my whole world had been turned upside down and I was starting to feel hopeful for the future again. If only Jet and Allie were with me. I missed my friends and I missed my family. It was hard to admit that I was enjoying my new life when I felt guilty about leaving behind everyone that I loved.

Sensing my troubled mind, the Queen asked me to join her for dinner. As we tucked into platters of fruit and nuts, warm spiced apple juice and sticky cinnamon sweets, I felt calmer and relaxed into my chair, hoping to hear some wise words from the Queen.

"You know LOLA, I was once a lot like you," she smiled.

"I'm not sure I like where this is going," I replied. "You mean you were hotheaded and always getting into trouble?"

"Not exactly... I mean I was unsure of myself and so I pretended to be tough so no one could hurt me. I see who you really are though, LOLA. I know how scared you were when you first arrived here and I can see you slowly starting to gain confidence in yourself and your abilities. I'm very proud of you, I thought you should know that," she said kindly.

"It's you I have to thank for all of it. I don't know what I would have done if I hadn't come here. I had no idea where I was going or what I was going to do," upon saying these words the truth of them started to sink in.

"Don't you see LOLA, you were destined to come here. Everything that should happen does happen eventually, don't you find?" she added with a grin.

"I still have so many questions, though. If this is my destiny, is it my town's destiny to be destroyed? How can I be so selfish? To fly off into the distance and leave them behind to face disaster?"

"Yes, but LOLA by leaving, you have at least opened up a door to something new. If you had stayed, do you think your warnings would have made any difference to them?" she asked.

"Well no, I tried and it got me into trouble," I answered.

"Then you had no choice but to do what you did. NOW the real question is knowing what you know, how can you help them?" she mused. I wasn't quite following her.

She continued, "With all your new skills and abilities, and of course some help from your new friends, do you think there's nothing you can do?" her eyes held mine and struck at the very core of me.

All of a sudden it was clear. How could I have not seen what she was doing? *Really LOLA, for a smart fairy sometimes you can be a little slow on the uptake,* I told myself.

All those lessons and all the practice, she was preparing me for battle! She was teaching me the skills I'd need to save my town.

<u>My New Mad Skills:</u>

Mindreading and communicating with other fairies and animals
Creating protective shields
Manipulating time
Affecting the weather
Glimmering, changing my appearance and the appearance of things around me
Spotting 'gifted' humans and communicating with them
Spotting 'unfriendly' humans and staying away from them
Making myself invisible
Affecting electrical currents and energy fields

That is a pretty impressive list; I think you'll agree!
But I had no idea what to do with it all...
"But where do we start? At the moment, all we really know is that something terrible is going to happen, but I don't know for sure WHAT it is or WHEN it will take place. That's not much to go on..." I told the Queen.
"You are not asking the right person. I don't have the gift of seeing the future, but that's why I took you to meet Reaya," replied the Queen.

"Reaya can see the future?" I asked incredulously.

"Absolutely, Reaya can see a set of events that will happen in the future. They can be changed of course, but that depends on what you do. So I suggest that you start by meeting with her tomorrow and then come back here and tell me what you find out."

It was going to be another long sleepless night.

THIRTEEN

JET GETS RECRUITED

Meanwhile back in the Blue Mountains, all was not well. LOLA's disappearance had caused a lot of trouble. The whole town was talking about it and the King had strictly forbidden her name to be mentioned.

The day LOLA left, the King had marched into the school and closed it down, claiming that the Headmaster was no longer fit to teach and that a replacement would be found. Until then, everyone was to be homeschooled. The Headmaster simply disappeared, and a week later the school was still boarded up with no news of a replacement anywhere in sight. All the other teachers were left without jobs, scratching their heads and wondering what to do.

Well you can imagine the chaos this caused.

Jet was not so bothered about the school being closed; he had other things on his mind. The day LOLA left, he'd been very angry. How could she do this to them, just drop them and then flee without even telling her best friends where she was going? If he'd known how everything would fall apart, he would have left with her, he knew that much.

To make matters worse, he hadn't seen Allie for a week now. He assumed her parents had grounded her and were keeping her locked inside, whenever he went to her house, her bedroom light was on but there was no sign of her. He had thrown stones at the window, whispered her name repeatedly day after day and she never came to the window. He had even knocked on the front door once or twice, but no one ever answered, not even her parents. She must be in a LOT of trouble, he knew that much.

Thankfully his parents had been quite reasonable considering everything. It turned out that they weren't big fans of the King and when he told them what had actually happened, they had taken his side and backed him up 100%. He wasn't grounded, but they had warned him not to get into any more trouble. In his Mother's words, "I don't trust that man, he's a power hungry so-and-so and it's best if you stay well clear of him, okay son?" she urged.

"Sure Mum," said Jet, grateful that his parents were being cool about things. The only good thing to come out of this whole mess was his new obsession. Becoming a Protector Fairy.

Ever since Jet had watched Mr. Holt throw that log off that wild pig, he'd been determined to find out more about him. The day the King closed down the school, Jet had followed Mr. Holt home and watched him for hours. It was just as he suspected, Mr. Holt was no normal teacher. From his vantage point up in the trees, Jet watched on in awe as Mr. Holt applied a glimmer to himself, and within seconds he changed appearance completely.

Gone was the shabby brown waistcoat and grey pants and in its place was what can only be described as a ninja outfit, complete with black leather pants, black combat boots and a silk black vest. His face and body changed too. He appeared younger and much stronger, his arm muscles rippled and his back and shoulders broadened out as he stretched out his wings to magnificent proportions. He suddenly filled the whole room and Jet had to clamp his mouth shut with his hand to make sure he didn't give himself away.

Then the strangest thing happened.

The room around Mr. Holt changed. A moment before, it had appeared like any other house, and then suddenly it was filled with light and movement like a thousand stars chasing each other in the darkness. Mr. Holt grabbed one of them and held it in front of his face at eye level. As he stared into the light, an image appeared. It was hard for Jet to see clearly what the image was, but it appeared to be a face and it seemed to be talking directly to Mr. Holt. Jet was too far away to hear what they were saying, but they were definitely having a conversation.

Now Jet was convinced he was right, this was not the kind of magic he had seen before. There was nothing else for it; he had to get closer so he could hear what was being said. Jet jumped down from his hiding spot and made a dash for the window to get a better look. As he reached the window, the face inside the light looked directly at him and then said something to Mr. Holt. Jet quickly ducked down out of view, but it was too late, he'd been spotted.

"What do you think you're doing spying on me, Jet?" asked Mr. Holt.

"Sorry Sir, I was just curious to see where you lived, I didn't mean to spy on you, I promise..." stuttered Jet.

"What did you see?" asked Mr. Holt.

"Nothing sir, although I can't help but notice that you've changed out of your school clothes. You look a lot cooler in that gear," ventured Jet.

Mr. Holt smiled at this, "Yes, well who says teachers have to look dull all of the time?"

"Quite right sir, although I don't think you're a regular teacher now are you?" Jet replied.

"What do you mean?" replied Mr. Holt.

"Sir, I saw you lift that log off that wild pig, remember? I know what you said happened, but I was there. It didn't just move because of the water, you threw it, I saw you do it. Now you can stick to that story if you like Sir, but considering what I just saw in your room, I'd say you're not a normal fairy."

"Is that right, well what do you think I am then?" asked Mr. Holt.

"A Protector Fairy sir, in fact I'm certain of it!" replied Jet.

"Hmm, a Protector Fairy you say. What do you actually know about them? As far as I'm aware, they haven't been legal for years," answered Mr. Holt.

"I don't know about legal, Sir. There's not much that IS legal around here anymore, but I've heard stories alright. I know enough to make me believe that it's possible that YOU are a Protector Fairy and that you're hiding it from everyone for some reason," answered Jet.

"Tell me something, assuming that I was a Protector Fairy, and I'm not admitting anything of the sort, BUT if I was a Protector Fairy, what would you do with that information?" asked Mr. Holt.

"I'd ask you to teach me everything you know, and of course I'd keep it 100% confidential, Sir. It's none of my business why you're hiding it!" said Jet.

"So you want to be a Protector Fairy, do you lad? I wonder if you know what you're asking?" replied Mr. Holt.

"Yes Sir, more than anything. I'm strong, the strongest in my class by far, and I'm fast and I don't quit—ever," Jet said proudly.

"That I don't doubt, I've seen you training at the gym and I can see how determined you are. BUT I wonder, are you ready for the rest of it? It's a lot of pressure being a Protector Fairy; often we are faced with situations where we or others may get injured, or even die. These are stressful times Jet, humans are destroying the planet and cutting down forests at an alarming rate. Our job is to protect fairies who are living all over the world. You have only ever lived in the Blue Mountains. Are you ready to travel, never knowing a home, never settling down, is this really the life for you? I urge you to think long and hard before you answer, Jet. Once you walk down this path, you can't change your mind," Mr. Holt said solemnly.

"I am certain of it," answered Jet bravely.

"In that case, we will start your training immediately, you've got a lot to learn and there is no time to waste. We can always find a place for a brave new recruit, welcome aboard Jet," said Mr. Holt, shaking his hand firmly.

RAISING AN ARMY

I was nervous going back to Reaya's house without the Queen. I shouldn't have been, she greeted me with the same warm smile and I was once again overwhelmed by the force and beauty of the silver aura floating around her like a second skin of glittering mist.

"LOLA, please come in and let's get started." She ushered me into the room. I came to a stop opposite her across a wooden table - Reaya sat elegantly on her chair as I hovered at her eye level. I waited while she tuned into whatever psychic energies she was able to access.

"So, LOLA, you came to ask me a question. Please go ahead when you are ready and I will do my best to answer you if I can," she stated matter-of-factly.

"Okay, well it's about my hometown in the Blue Mountains..." I continued to fill her in on what I'd overheard at school, what I'd learned about the disaster in 1985, and finally my fears that the community was in danger again and I didn't know how to help them...

She was quiet for what seemed like hours, but in reality it was probably five minutes. Her eyes were closed and her face was impossible to read.

It was torture.

Finally she opened her eyes and I saw her brush aside a flicker of distress.

"I'm afraid I understand now what brought you to me LOLA, there is indeed a future that holds much sadness in the Blue Mountains. I see blindness and arrogance and fear blanketing the town like a dark cloud. I see warnings that no one heeds and I see pain and death for many and then finally sorrow and regret..." She sighed, and I could tell that whatever she was seeing was hard to watch.

"But is there a future where this doesn't happen, is there any way I can stop it?" I asked.

"Well of course LOLA, there are always many future realities for any situation. I see a set of events based on what is *most likely* to happen if things stay on their current path,

HOWEVER if something or someone were to upset the events leading up to this, then yes, a new future can appear in its place," she answered.

"Do you know what day it will happen? How accurate can you be?" This felt like the most important question.

"I can't see an exact date, I'm sorry. But I can tell you it will be soon, before this month ends. The visions are very strong and they only appear this clearly to me when it is close to the time," she replied.

"Okay thanks Reaya, you've been a great help. I'm going to go and tell the Queen everything you've said. If you're right, we don't have a minute to waste!" I was frantic now with worry, my worst fears had been confirmed and I had no choice but to act.

The Queen was waiting for me when I returned. She patiently listened as I repeated everything Reaya had told me, and once I'd finished she simply stood up and walked away.

I was confused by her reaction, had I done something wrong, was history repeating itself? I sat dumbstruck and was starting to think the worst again, that she didn't believe me, and I would have to face the challenge alone...

What I saw next bowled me over. The Queen strode majestically towards me and I could see a long line of fierce Water Fairies walking behind her in pairs. Each fairy had their arms raised in solidarity and I realized that the Queen *hadn't* deserted me at all, she'd gone to gather an army to fight with me!

I'd never felt such love for another fairy in my life, all the fear drained from me and I jumped up and cheered. I was not alone, these beautiful magical creatures would stand side by side with me, and the powerful Queen of the Water Fairies was leading the charge.

"We will fly tonight!" she cried with her arm raised and her hair glowing in the dusk light.

The Water Fairies roared their approval. I looked on with pride and joined in with their fierce battle cries. It was time to face whatever lay ahead of us, but I saw no fear on their faces, I saw friendship and strength, and above all hope.

I woke before dawn, anxious to start the day and face whatever lay ahead. I was nervous, but my new friends had restored my faith and I felt stronger in their presence. I thought about my friends and family back home, I wondered if they had any idea what was coming or if they even wondered where I'd gone. I hoped that they hadn't forgotten about me, or worse still, that they were glad I was gone and could cause them no more trouble.

As the sun rose, I could hear signs of life in the cave. Fairies were waking and beginning the day. I ventured out into the main cave with a steely determination and a thousand butterflies in my stomach. I forced myself to eat; I would need my strength for the journey back to the Blue Mountains and whatever was waiting there for us. Reaya had predicted that the threat was coming soon, so that could mean any day now as there were only six more days left in the month. I figured it would take us the best part of a day to travel and I hoped that we wouldn't be too late.

"Gather around everyone," called the Queen.

"Today, we join our new friend LOLA on a journey. We do not know what we will face when we get there, but we need to be prepared to use all of our powers to keep her friends and loved ones safe. We will split into three groups and I will nominate a leader for each group. LOLA will take the first group and lead the way as she has made the journey before. Do you think you can remember the way, LOLA?" she asked me.

"Yes, I believe I can," I replied, more confidently than I actually felt.

"Okay good, you will lead the first group then," she said. "Paige and Eva will take the second group, and Banjo you will join me in leading the last group. We must make sure that no one gets lost or left behind. I suggest everyone who hasn't eaten a good breakfast does so now, we will leave in 30 minutes."

It was a beautiful day, perfect for flying, and I took this to be a good sign. A storm or heavy rain would have affected our flying time, so this was a most lucky beginning.

We left the cave in our groups. I led the way out into the brilliant sunshine and was met by a welcome sight. The swallows that had guided me to Katia and her community were waiting for us in the dancing tree. They swooped down and joined me at the front of the pack.

"You didn't think we'd let you fly alone, did you?" asked Tilda.

"But how did you know?" I asked her in surprise.

"A little bird told me," she replied, and she exchanged a knowing glance with Katia the Queen of the Water Fairies.

I was filled with gratitude to the Queen and to my fine feathered friends for their help. Truthfully, I was a little nervous of leading the way. They had helped me find my way to Byron Bay and even though I thought I knew my way back, there was a tiny seed of doubt in my mind. That doubt was now gone. With Tilda, Marty and Misty leading the way, we'd be back in the Blue Mountains in no time at all.

And then we were off.

If anyone had been paying close attention as we started our journey - three hundred fairies and three swallows flying across the sky - they would have thought we were quite a sight. We stayed tightly packed in our groups, with me at the front and the swallows right by my side.

We began our journey across the coast, staying low in amongst the reeds and the bushes, skimming the sea in a flash of brilliant colours. We flew for hours without rest; we passed towns and villages, beaches and fields that stretched for miles before we finally saw the landscape change and the mountains become taller and the valleys deeper. We were getting closer.

The landscape of the Blue Mountains was unmistakable, with deep lush forest surrounded by tall craggy mountains. I was overcome with a longing for my home that I hadn't allowed myself to feel until then. The closer we got, the stronger the pull was and I could clearly see the faces of Jet and Allie in my mind.

This gave me a new found determination, and I dug deeper than ever before and flew as if my life depended on it. The others could sense the change in me and they matched my speed. Even the younger fairies did not disappoint. This journey was asking a lot of even the strongest most experienced flyers, and yet there was no one straggling behind or grumbling to take a break. I was so proud of them all and grateful for such fine new friends.

We arrived just before sunset. As we approached the outskirts of my hometown, I began to feel nervous and I signaled to the others to slow down as we were nearing our destination. I also wasn't sure how we would be greeted. I wondered, should I face everyone now and tell them everything I'd learned in hopes they believed me, or was it best to watch and wait? The Queen, sensing my uncertainty, was quick to suggest that we should rest and make our plans in the morning. I was relieved, although it was hard not to shout it from the rooftops (like the old LOLA would have done). My journey had taught me that sometimes it's better to sit back and consider the options carefully before acting. The Queen and her calm influence seemed to be rubbing off on me!

We found shelter in the side of a mossy bank; here we found a fallen tree that created a perfect hideout for us. It was a very secluded spot that I'd never been to before, so I felt certain that we would be safe there until morning. We were tired from the flight and after a meal of berries and fresh green leaves, sleep came easily to us all. As I drifted off into my dreams, I let my aching body relax into the mossy bed and hoped and prayed for a happy ending to my story.

THE POWER OF JET

Jet had been hard at work. Never before had he applied himself to a task with such focus. Mr. Holt was an awesome teacher, and it turned out, there was a LOT to learn. According to Mr. Holt, every fairy had the ability to do amazing things, but for some reason the King had decided to keep these skills a secret from everyone.

Jet could hardly believe his eyes as Mr. Holt showed him how to focus his energy on moving objects. He imagined giant flashes of electricity pouring out of his hands and pushing objects away from him. At first, he practiced on small things, like nuts and leaves, and then as he got better he was able to move huge rocks and even a fallen log! That was obviously how Mr. Holt had moved a log from the wild pig.

Once he had mastered moving objects with his energy fields, he learned how to create protective shields around himself and Mr. Holt by imagining a force field of brilliant white light surrounding them both. He could hardly believe what was happening as he watched the force field get stronger and clearer as his confidence grew. And finally, he learned how to talk to other Protector Fairies in far off lands. The scene he had witnessed in Mr. Holt's house had been something to behold, but to actually do this himself was even more impressive. He sat and talked to a whole community of Protector Fairies working in the African desert. He heard them tell tales of their heroic adventures around the world, and became even more certain that this was what he wanted to do with his life.

Jet was a natural at anything physical, which was no real surprise, but as his lessons got tougher and tougher, Jet began to realize just how much more he had to learn.

After one very successful day of training, Mr. Holt asked Jet to sit with him and talk for a while.

"Jet I need to tell you something. I haven't been entirely honest with you," began Mr. Holt.

"Erm, okay," said Jet wondering where this was going.

"The day you came to spy on me, it wasn't unexpected. I knew you were coming and I wanted you to find me," said Mr. Holt.

Jet was silent, not quite sure what he was supposed to say.

"I came to the school for a reason, Jet, and I think you've always known this. I wanted you to find me and I wanted to recruit you," he added.

"But why haven't you said anything this whole time and why tell me now?" asked Jet, slightly annoyed.

"I was waiting until I was sure that you were ready, and today I am certain that you are. You've been patient and followed my instructions perfectly and I have to admit that I've never seen a fairy learn as quickly as you and demonstrate such raw power. However, I'm afraid it seems that time is not on our side. I've been told that danger is coming any day now, so I have to warn you that you will be tested like you've never been tested. I wanted to teach you everything I know, but I am confident that you know enough to stand by me and fight. Help is coming any day now; there is word of a fairy army headed towards us as we speak. We will join forces with them and face whatever lies ahead. Are you with me Jet?" asked Mr. Holt.

Jet had never been so sure of anything in his life.

SIXTEEN

THERE IS STRENGTH IN NUMBERS

Katia the Queen of the Water Fairies was the first to wake. She shook me urgently and whispered that I had to get up. I looked around to see Paige waking everyone up just as urgently, and I got a wave of dread as I noticed the grimace on the faces of Paige and the Queen.

"I've heard from Reaya," announced the Queen. "I'm afraid it is as we feared, the attack will happen soon. We must go now."

I was momentarily struck dumb. Despite everything, even after seeing Reaya and hearing for myself her prophecy that confirmed my worst fears, I still held out a flicker of hope that it wasn't real. Now the moment was here. One thing was for certain, we would be tested today, and whilst I desperately hoped we would be victorious, I was terrified that we would fail.

Once the news had sunk in, there was a flurry of activity. The Queen began circling the fairies, whispering to them and giving out instructions. I led the way with the Queen at my side. I felt a new found courage as I looked back and saw the strength of our numbers.

As we neared my old home, the Queen instructed us to approach carefully and look for any signs of a disturbance. I knew the lay of the land, so it was my job to assess if there was anything out of the ordinary. All looked eerily quiet as we arrived. There was no sign of life at all, and I had a sense of dread that we were too late. Gradually it dawned on me that it was just before sunrise and no one would be awake yet. I was so nervous that I hadn't realized how early the Queen had woken us - I breathed a sigh of relief as I saw lights glimmering in the windows of my home and peered into the other houses to see the same.

"All looks clear," I informed the Queen.

"Okay, so we have some time. LOLA, do you have any friends nearby who you can trust with your life? This is very important, so you need to be sure..."

"Yes, Jet and Allie. They are the only people who believed me in the first place, and they are my best friends, I can trust them with anything," I assured her.

"Good, well we are going to need some friends on the inside. If there is an attack today, we will need someone to evacuate the town. Reaya said someone would be here to join our fight, so we must assume it's your friends. Our job is to protect it from the outside and hopefully stop the attack from happening, BUT if things go wrong, we will need to get everyone to safety and quickly," she added.

"I will go and talk to them," I said, "you stay here and keep an eye out and I'll be as quick as I can," I promised.

"LOLA, use your invisibility power, just to be safe," she urged.

"I'd forgotten about that, good idea," I replied. It was time to put my new skills to the test. I had a little giggle to myself thinking that Jet and Allie would be stunned by my new powers and I couldn't wait to teach them everything I'd learned!

I concentrated hard and after a few false starts, I successfully made myself disappear. I still had to pinch myself whenever I did this - it's a weird feeling being there, but not being there, if you know what I mean.

I headed to Jet's house first. As I approached, I could see early signs of rising. His Mum was in the kitchen preparing breakfast and his little brother was happily buzzing around her feet. I found Jet in his room; he seemed to be preparing for training as he was dressed in his combat gear. I didn't want to scare him so I whispered from outside the window.

"Jet it's me, open up."

"LOLA, is that you? Where have you been, I've been going out of my mind?!" he peered out the window looking for me, but of course he couldn't see me. I decided to have a little fun with it.

"I'm right here," I giggled.

"Stop messing around LOLA, I've been so worried, where are you hiding?" I was two feet in front of him as I waved off my invisibility charm.

"What the?..." shouted Jet.

"Shhhh, I don't want anyone to know I'm here," I whispered urgently.

"LOLA, how did you do that? One minute you weren't there, and then the next you're right in front of me. How DID you do that?" he asked incredulously.

"I'll tell you all about it later, for now I need you to listen to me as we don't have much time," I urged.

"I know," said Jet.

"It's all real Jet, everything we suspected, it's going to happen. Maybe even today, and I need your help," I added. Jet just smiled. "Hang on, did you just say I know?" I asked.

"Yes LOLA, I've got heaps to tell you as well. I haven't just been sitting here twiddling my thumbs you know, but first you need to tell me what the plan is and what you need me to do. I assume this has something to do with the fairy army you've got with you, am I right?" asked Jet smugly.

"Okay, I'm not going to ask how you know that, frankly I don't care. So you're in then, you're ready to fight against whatever it is that we're up against?" I asked.

"You can count on me, LOLA. I've got mad new skills that I'm ready to show off, thanks to Mr. Holt, and I'm assuming by what I just saw that you've got some of your own, am I right?" asked Jet.

"You sure are buddy, you wait until I show you my moves. You're a good friend Jet, I've missed you." I hugged him and laughed.

"Okay, so what's the plan boss?"

"I need you to go and get Allie and meet me by the main road into town. There's a small brook just to the left that's covered by a fallen pine tree. I'll be waiting there for you. Don't tell anyone you've seen me, not even Allie," I insisted.

"We might have a problem there," replied Jet.

"What do you mean?" I asked.

"No one has seen Allie since the day you left... I've been at her house every day, but her parents won't answer the door. The light in her room is on, but no matter how many times I've knocked on her window, she never answers. It's weird, I think she must be grounded for life or her parents have locked her up or something!"

"Oh no, poor Allie, I can't believe I got her into so much trouble," I replied, feeling like an awful friend.

"I know, I feel terrible too. We'll have some serious groveling to do once this is all over," he added.

"You're not wrong. In the meantime, you said something about Mr. Holt. Does that mean you were right and he's not a normal teacher?" I asked hopefully.

"You need to see it to believe it, LOLA. He IS a Protector Fairy, and a pretty cool one too as it turns out. He is the one who's been training me since you've been gone. Don't worry, he's on our side. I'll go and get him and we can worry about Allie once this is all over. I know her parents will see sense when we show them that we were right to raise the alarm."

"Okay, so I'll meet you by the main road into town then, yes?" I shouted as I flew off to join my army of Water Fairies.

"You can count on me LOLA!" shouted Jet in reply.

I didn't want to risk being seen, so I cast my invisibility charm again, and for good measure I added a protective shield around myself so I could fly completely undetected and unharmed.

The Queen and her faithful army of Water Fairies were nervously waiting for me and breathed a sigh of relief when I made myself appear in the middle of them.

"Ah LOLA, welcome back. How did it go? Did you see your friends, did anyone spot you?" asked the Queen.

"It was fine, I saw Jet and it turns out that HE is the 'help' that Reaya was talking about. It's amazing, he's been training with Mr. Holt - who it turns out is a Protector Fairy - and they are going to join us in our fight! My friend Allie is nowhere to be seen though, we think her parents have her locked up for all the trouble we caused. But I can't do anything about that until we prove we were right all along. I used my invisibility charm, so I'm certain no one saw me," I assured her. "What about here, have you seen anything unusual?"

"Well, it's hard to say. We're not from here so we don't know what is normal. We saw a few big trucks go past just a minute ago, but they had no signs on them so I'm not sure what they were carrying. Other than that, there was not much traffic on the road," she replied.

Hmmm, trucks I thought, they could be farmers or food delivery trucks. Humans often deliver food early in the morning for the farmers markets and little stores and cafes. I decided it didn't sound like much of a threat, so I took my position by their side watching the main road.

"I think we should split up," the Queen announced.

"We don't know for sure if the humans will travel by main road, best to keep an eye on all the roads into the town," she added thoughtfully.

"Agreed, I'll stay here and wait for Jet and Mr. Holt. Paige and her group can wait with me, if you can lead groups to cover the other roads in and do some loops around the area just to be safe."

"Sounds like a plan," said the Queen as she quickly organized her teams into smaller troops and gave them their instructions.

I waited for what seemed like hours, all was quiet and there was nothing that even suggested a threat, so I was starting to get bored. All of a sudden, Jet and Mr. Holt zoomed over the hills towards me. At first I thought they were just excited to see us and I rushed to meet them with a huge grin on my face. But as they got closer, I saw that neither of them was smiling, in fact they both wore very dark expressions on their faces.

"What, what is it?" I shouted to them.

Jet spoke up first, "Just when we were leaving to meet you, we heard a loud noise, the sound of metal banging and an unusual amount of humans talking. I'm not quite sure what we saw, but it looked like a huge dome was being built, there were at least twenty humans there. I don't like the look of them LOLA, they weren't locals, I know that much," he insisted.

"Where were they?"

"That's the worrying part, they were right by our underground tunnels. NO humans ever go near there, that's why we stopped to check it out. Mr. Holt's house is right at the back on the other side of the tree, so we were able to watch without being seen... they were right by the main entrance near the Royal Grounds," he added.

"Okay, I need to warn the others and we need to send a team to investigate," I replied.

"What others, who is here with you?" Jet asked.

"Oh sorry, I forgot to introduce you, I was so excited to see you that I nearly forgot my manners," I apologized.

"Come out guys, it's all cool, I'd like you to meet some friends of mine."

The Water Fairies (who'd been politely staying out of sight) rushed forward and introduced themselves to Jet and Mr. Holt.

"Whoa, this is crazy LOLA, I know you said you had an army but I didn't realize there would be this many fairies. Where did you find so many?" asked Jet, his eyes almost popping out of his head.

"This is only a third of them, wait until you meet the Queen as well, she'll blow your mind!" I exclaimed excitedly.

"The Queen, wait do you mean? *Our* Queen?" asked Jet.

"No, not our Queen. I've been living with the Water Fairies in Byron Bay and *their* Queen is leading the army that's here to help us," I replied proudly. "We've got so much catching up to do, but all you need to know is that they are my friends, and they are here to help us fight whatever is threatening us. The Queen and the rest of the Water Fairies are currently guarding the roads and doing sweeps of the town, but right now I need to alert them to what you've seen, Jet. Give me a minute whilst I talk to her."

And with that I closed my eyes and projected an image of the scene Jet had described just minutes before into the mind of the Queen. I was hopeful she'd get my message and return quickly.

"So I see that someone has taught you how to use your powers, LOLA!" said Mr. Holt, suitably impressed by what he'd seen.

"You won't believe it sir, I can hardly believe it myself. The Queen and my new friends Paige, Eva and Banjo taught me to use ALL of my magical powers. There's so much we weren't taught, but it sounds like you've been helping Jet to do the same," I replied.

"You don't need to call me Sir anymore, LOLA," laughed Mr. Holt. "Plain old Thomas is fine, we're on the same team now and what matters is that we use everything we've got to keep everyone safe, don't you agree?" he asked.

"100% Sir, oops I mean Thomas. It might take me a while to get used to that," I giggled in return. As if on cue, the Queen and three hundred Water Fairies flew in and surrounded us.

Jet and Mr. Holt stumbled backwards slightly and turned to look at me with impressed smiles plastered on their faces.

"Ah you must be Jet, and let me see, you must be the Protector Fairy I've been hearing all about. Thomas Holt, if I'm not mistaken?" guessed the Queen quite correctly.

"I am indeed, and you must be Katia the Queen of the Water Fairies," replied Mr. Holt as he bent to kiss Katia gallantly on the hand.

"LOLA just shared a vision with me. Have you ever seen those humans before and could you tell what they were building? The image projected looked like a plastic dome on a metal frame, is that what you saw?" she asked him.

"No, I've never seen them before. No one comes near our underground homes normally, as they are very well hidden.

The King chose that spot especially for its privacy. We see maybe one or two humans a day within a mile of us, and that's a busy day!" answered Jet earnestly.

"Okay, so I think we need to assume that this is not good news," said the Queen.

Just as she spoke, we heard a strong rumble coming over the hill. We all peered up and saw a line of trucks, vans and cars coming into town in quick succession. The Queen turned to me and we exchanged a knowing look.

This was it. Whatever IT was, was headed our way now and we knew it had something to do with the dome. Mention of the dome had struck a distant chord in my memory; I could swear that the caretaker had mentioned a dome was involved in the events of 1985, could history really be repeating itself?

"Thomas and Jet, you need to get into the town and start evacuating people. I don't care what you tell people, just get them out of there by the back houses as quickly as possible. Don't use the main entrance if that's where the humans are positioned," I ordered them.

"And be careful, we have no idea what these humans are doing or how dangerous they are, so don't get caught, okay?" I added.

"Got it LOLA, don't worry, we'll get them out safely," insisted Jet with a determined look on his face.

"LOLA you come with me," said the Queen. "We're going straight to the source. We'll go and see what this dome is and find out what they are intending to do with it. Before we go, we need to split everyone up into groups. They will have to throw everything they've got at those trucks and vans that are headed this way. I think it might be time for an electrical storm in the Blue Mountains, that will slow them down a bit, what do you think Mr. Holt?" she asked him with a glint in her eye.

"I think you're absolutely right. There's nothing like a good storm to make humans jumpy," he replied, laughing heartily.

We raced off, confident in the abilities of our fairy army to stir up an almighty storm that would slow down the new arrivals. Other fairies were told to raise the alarm with as many local animals and insects as they could reach. We needed numbers and we hoped they would answer our call for help.

I set off with the Queen in the direction of the Royal Grounds and the opening to our underground homes. There were about 250 homes nestled under that large tree and the (now closed down) school was nearby. Our entire community lived in an area no bigger than a large duck pond.

As we flew above the trees, we looked down and spotted the dome that Jet had told us about, only now it was completely built. It stood fifteen feet tall and was entirely covering the Royal Grounds, the school and the entrance to the underground tunnel.

A terrible thought entered my mind, what if we were too late? Whatever this dome was, it was completely blocking our entrance and I could see no way of breaking through. The only hope was the back way into the tunnel, where I prayed Mr. Holt and Jet were helping the townsfolk escape.

The Queen raised her arm and told us to stop, and we all hovered in midair, uncertain what to do next. I scanned the ground below desperately looking for any sign of Jet or Mr. Holt. I could see a swarm of frightened fairies frantically trying to escape from the dome. They were beating themselves up against the plastic interior of the walls and flying up to the top trying to find an opening. I ignored the Queen and made a beeline for the top of the dome, desperate to try and break through and free them. I could hear their screams as I circled above them, unable to find a way in.

"LOLA, remember what I told you. Trust your instincts, be calm and the answer will appear!" the Queen shouted up to me. I looked at her in frustration, why wasn't she doing anything? This was like a bad dream, we were three hundred strong and yet we couldn't break through one stupid plastic

130

dome. What use were all my powers if I couldn't use them to help my friends? I had to STOP this!

And then time stopped. The world ceased spinning, and the scene below became a freeze frame like a picture. I could see the open mouths of my fairy friends below, their cries frozen mid scream. The leaves on the trees stopped rustling, the humans were turned to statues below me and yet the Queen and her Water Fairy army were completely unaffected.

"Oh well done LOLA, you've frozen time, was that you?" she laughed jubilantly.

"Well I don't think so, I just wanted it to stop and then it did. Could that be... was that really me?" I asked hesitantly.

"Well I didn't do it. I didn't even think of that to be honest, I was too busy trying to think of a way to break through the dome. This will give us the advantage, it will give us time to check the dome and see if there are any weak spots. Just concentrate on what you're doing, keep time frozen whilst I look for a way to break through. Also, I want to get a good look at what the humans are doing, maybe it will tell us why they are here in the first place!" she shouted.

I concentrated on stopping what I was seeing below. I had one intention, and one intention only. This would not happen on my watch. As I held my mind steady, I watched as the Queen and Paige did laps of the dome. Some of the humans were in strange outfits, like spacesuits. They were carrying clipboards and I could see Paige straining to read their minds. It's harder for a fairy to read the mind of a human, but Paige was an expert at mind reading - if anyone could understand their jumbled thoughts, it would be her.

I lost my train of thought and before I knew it, the scene below me had come back to life. I was tired from concentrating so hard and I tried again, but it was no use. Unsure what to do next, I looked to the Queen for help.

"They are doing some type of scientific study of the land, something to do with gas mining apparently. As far as I can tell, they had no idea that there was a fairy community living here. It's a most unfortunate coincidence that they chose to study this area of land. The human minds I could read clearly seem completely confused by what they have found. But now that they've stumbled across what is clearly a miniature community with a Royal Palace and everything, you can be sure that they will be capturing the fairies that live here. I'd be very surprised if anyone makes it out alive," Paige informed us.

"This could have all been avoided by the King!" screamed the Queen. "All he needed to do was communicate with the local humans. Everyone knows that there are plenty of magical people in the Blue Mountains, they would have warned him of this and there would have been plenty of time to evacuate!" Katia was furious at the King's reluctance to use his powers for the protection of his own people.

His ignorance had cost them dearly. If he, like the Queen of the Water Fairies, had friends like Reaya, he would have been warned about the danger with plenty of time to spare. He could have moved the community to another site and they could have built again. Yes it would take time, but at least they would be safe! I wondered now if Mr. Holt had a friend like Reaya too. He had obviously come to protect us, and yet no one had listened to him either.

"There's only one thing for it," said the Queen, "we need to distract them. We need to cause a disturbance so almighty that the humans will stop their tasks. Then we can go in and rescue those poor fairies that are trapped inside."

"How do you propose we do that?" I asked. As I uttered those words, a dark swarm approached. It was so huge and swift moving that it took us a while to work out what it was. The rest of the fairy army had arrived and they had company - butterflies, bees, wasps, beetles and dragonflies swarmed into view, closely followed by flocks of birds so dense and in such quick succession that they appeared like a huge black cloud covering the sun. On the ground, I heard the welcome sounds of wild pigs, possums, lizards and echidnas thundering through the bush followed by beavers, badgers and mice. I'd never seen such a wonderful sight; the animals and insects had heard our calls for help and were here in the thousands.

Inside the dome, some of the humans were carrying on despite the distractions. They were digging up our homes and attacking the walls of the Palace to see what was inside. We watched on in horror, as fairies fled from the tunnels, trying to find an escape route. They flew straight into the walls of the dome, trapped and terrified by what was happening around them.

We all knew what to do without even discussing it - our instincts were kicking in. It was now or never. A group of the younger Water Fairies concentrated all their powers on affecting the weather and within minutes the storm that was passing over the town (created originally to see off the vans and trucks) was now whistling its way into view. Dark thunderous clouds rolled and clapped above us and torrential rain poured from the sky, causing a great blue mist to settle on the tree tops of the Blue Mountains.

Lighting struck at the very foundations of the dome and made all the humans jump in fright. They were definitely unsettled by the weather, but so far it wasn't forcing them to leave the dome. They seemed determined to continue their destruction, no matter what chaos went on around them. I was starting to lose faith when a huge lightning bolt hit the truck to the right of the dome. This seemed to get their attention. Five of the humans left the dome to survey the damage and stare at the wild weather, wondering where it had come from. Just minutes before, it had been clear blue skies and sunny, and now the sky was full of dark clouds and loud claps of thunder.

I scanned the ground looking for Jet and Mr. Holt again, still no sign. Where could they be, I wondered? I could see Paige and Eva off in the distance helping groups of trapped fairies escape through the underground tunnels. I could see Katia helping the younger fairies whip up the mighty storm, but there was just no sign of Mr. Holt and Jet. I tried to use my mental powers to lock on to their position, but it was too cloudy and unclear. For some reason, I kept seeing Allie's face but that made no sense at all.

The sounds from below jolted me out of my trance. Down on the ground, the force of the animal army was being felt. The animals were running straight at the dome in a frenzied effort to break through. They were head butting, biting and kicking at the edges. It was an impressive effort and it took the humans by complete surprise. The smaller animals forced their way past the terrified humans and entered the dome. They scratched and nipped at the feet of the humans, making them jump and lash out in frustration.

The swarm of fairies and insects went to work, led by Banjo and his friends. The brave fairies camouflaged themselves to look like bees and wasps - this was a clever strategy making them appear fierce and able to sting, but also concealing their true identities. I watched on with pride as Banjo and his friends went to work attacking the humans, stinging them over and over on their faces and their hands. This was exactly the distraction we needed. The humans were now fleeing the dome in droves, some of them were screaming and others were jumping about madly trying to swat at their attackers.

We had to move now whilst they were on the run.

Then a thought hit me, it was a phrase that the Queen had told me when I first arrived in Byron Bay.

There is strength in numbers, LOLA; we must work together to overcome obstacles.

What if all the fairies, all the animals and the insects pushed in the same direction at the wall of the dome at the same time? Could they topple it, would it be enough? The Queen had heard my thoughts...

"Yes LOLA, yes it's worth a try! Quickly, we must tell them now, whilst we have the advantage."

The Queen and I stood shoulder-to-shoulder, projecting our commands to the throng of fairies, animals and insects below. They all stopped in their tracks and listened intently, then they nodded and the great push began.

As soon as they surged, the humans paid attention. The sight of a thousand angry animals and insects coming right at them must have been quite scary. I saw two of them run to the van and take out what looked like guns.

"Not on my watch you don't," I screamed, filled with rage. I turned my attention to the humans holding the guns and focusing with all my might, I stopped them dead in their tracks. I zoned in on them, and them alone, and turned them to concrete. They stood fixed like toy soldiers to the ground as the other scientists watched on in horror. As the brave fairy army continued to push and shove at the dome with all their might, I held my gaze solely on the humans holding the guns. There was no way they could even fire one shot whilst I kept them frozen in time.

Lightening struck, thunder roared, animals huffed and grunted in the strain and eventually the dome began to tip and shake. The movement set off a new wave of excitement amongst the army, and they pushed and shoved with all their might. Out of nowhere Mr. Holt suddenly appeared and joined in the fight. If Jet was right and he had the strength of ten fairies, then he would be a welcome addition to the valiant warriors. I watched as he extended his wings to full length and dive bombed straight into the faces of the startled humans - cutting them over and over again with the sharp blades of his wings.

Flashes of electric blue light streamed from his hands and picked up rocks that he flung furiously at our attackers. He used their own tools against them, sending spades and lanterns flying through the air to hit them repeatedly until they cowered in the corner.

With one final push, the wall to the dome finally collapsed to the ground. The animals, insects and fairies all spilled out onto the grass, exhausted but triumphant. The humans, who were defeated, bruised, cut and covered in bee stings, finally retreated into their vans and sped off with their two frozen friends. All that was left was a broken dome, tattered in pieces on the ground, and the almighty mess that they left behind of what was once our town.

When the danger was over, we all collapsed into a heap on the ground and looked around at the damage. The Water Fairies gathered in small groups to talk excitedly about all they had seen and done. The fairies from my hometown sat in shock, they were still trying to grasp what had happened to them. Even though they were grateful to be alive, they were terribly upset about losing their homes and were nervously discussing what to do next. Many of them were injured or in shock. Groups of Water Fairies rushed around tending to the sick, fixing their injuries with healing charms and trying to give comfort to the scared younger fairies.

Despite my exhaustion, I was anxious to find my friends and my parents. I still hadn't seen Jet, and there had been no sign of Allie since I had left the Blue Mountains! Now that the immediate danger was over, I had to find her. I hoped that she was somewhere safe with Jet, so went off in search of them.

I flew over what remained of our town, scanning every underground house, broken tree stump and piece of rubble, but I found nothing at all. There was no sign of life. Just as before, I was stopped in my tracks by the image of Allie's face, but this time it was crystal clear. She was crying, and she looked scared. I could hear Jet's voice shouting to me and I frantically tried to work out where the shouts were coming from. And then I saw it, she was trapped in a dark room and was covered in rocks and mud and dust. I could see Jet lifting huge pieces of rubble from on top of her. She was crouched underneath looking scared to death. I shouted out hoping they could hear me.

"Jet, Allie, where are you? I can't see you...I'm coming," I told them as I frantically buzzed around trying to get a grip on where the sounds were coming from. Mr. Holt was by my side in a flash, "The Palace, LOLA," he shouted, "the sounds are coming from inside the Palace!" And he took off towards what remained of the once great Palace.

"But there's nothing left of it!" I screamed to him.

"It's definitely the Palace, LOLA. You take the far side and I'll take the front entrance. They must be trapped somewhere inside," he assured me. "Don't worry, we'll find them!" And with that, he flew off towards the main entrance.

I had never moved so quickly in my life. If they were inside the Palace, it could collapse at any minute, and there was no time to waste. As I reached the back of the crumbling walls, I finally saw movement. Jet was throwing rocks off into the distance. They were huge, but for each rock he threw away, another one seemed to roll down to replace it.

"She's inside LOLA, quick Allie is trapped inside!" he shouted. 'The King has had her locked up for over a week now. When I find him, I will kill him!" he said, furious with rage.

"Oh no, Allie!" I rushed to his side to help, but it seemed like nothing we did was helping. Every second that passed by, more and more rocks fell and the space that Allie was crouched in was filling up with rocks and mud at an alarming rate.

I stopped and concentrated hard. If I could just put a protective shield around Allie, it would give us the time we needed to get more help and break her out.

"What are you doing?" cried Jet. "Don't stop, we're going to lose her."

"I promise I know what I'm doing Jet, give me a minute." I closed my eyes and imagined a huge ball of white light. I strengthened it, adding layer after layer and making it bigger and stronger with each breath I took into my body. I focused on an image of Allie, her face scared and tear lined, and I forced the white ball of light around her, imagining it as a strong wall protecting her from harm.

"Nice work LOLA, I didn't think of that," said Jet, and he added extra layers to the shield using his own powers. Together we made an awesome team.

I opened my eyes and saw a huge glowing ball of light surrounding our friend as she peered up at us with her big eyes full of wonder.

"Just keep moving those rocks, Jet. I'm going to get Mr. Holt and the others to help," I promised him.

Without having to utter a word, Mr. Holt and Katia appeared, followed by at least a hundred fairies.

"We heard you LOLA, we're here. Don't you worry Allie, we'll have you out of there in no time at all," they assured her.

They set to work clearing away the piles of rocks that were trapping Allie underground, all while the protective shield that Jet and I concentrated on kept Allie safe from harm. Eventually, there was a gap big enough to reach her and I pulled her out to safety. I then gave her the biggest bear hug imaginable. Jet joined in, huffing and puffing after his super fairy efforts.

"Hey guys, I nearly got crushed to death in there, do you think you can give me a minute to catch my breath?" She laughed at us.

"Sorry, Allie," said Jet. "We're just so happy that you're okay," he told her.

"Thanks to you guys, I am now," she beamed.

"What were you doing in there anyway?" I asked her. "Why did the King lock you up?"

"His precious daughter, that's why. It turns out she made such a fuss about the dress I made that she just HAD to have it," she answered us.

"But why did he lock you up for that?" I asked.

"Because he's a mean and miserable King. He didn't want anyone to know that I made the dress because we insulted him and everything. So he told my parents that I had to 'do my duty' for the King and no one could know about it. Can you believe that?" she cried.

"I still don't get it, why didn't your parents say no?" I knew Allie's parents and I couldn't understand why they would let the King get away with this.

"He threatened them. He said he would banish them from the town and take away our house. My parents were devastated; they didn't know what to do so they hid from everyone and kept quiet. It was only meant to be for a week and they didn't know that I was locked in a room. He told them that I'd be treated like a guest. Huh, fat chance!" replied Allie.

"The nerve of that guy. I can't believe it, all of this is his fault!" I said to no one in particular.

"Well you're safe now Allie, and you can be sure the King will get what's coming to him, don't you worry about that," said Mr. Holt firmly.

We made our way back to the rest of the fairies who were waiting nervously for news of Allie. I could see my parents pacing up and down anxiously, and Allie's parents were sitting cuddling each other with terrified looks on their faces. As we rounded the corner of the Palace grounds, their eyes lit up upon seeing their daughter and they rushed to be by her side. My own parents stopped dead in their tracks when they saw us and waved madly at me.

I approached gingerly. I wasn't sure whether they would be pleased to see me or not, considering I'd run away and everything.

"Oh LOLA, we were so scared when you went missing. Thank goodness you are home safe. And we are so proud of you. Mr. Holt told us that this is all your doing, you brought everyone to help us!" cried my Mum, hugging me harder than I'd ever been hugged before.

"I know I shouldn't have run away, and I'm really sorry that I made you worry, but I can't explain it. I just knew that something terrible was going to happen and I couldn't just stay and watch it..." I hoped she understood.

"And a good job too, if you ask me. We were wrong, LOLA, we should have trusted you, we should have believed in you. We let you down," said my Dad regretfully.

At that moment, I felt like my heart would burst. Everyone I loved was safe, my family had welcomed me back and there was new hope for the future.

The Queen was watching on smiling as I reconciled with my parents. I had so much to thank her for, she had given me the strength to believe in myself and she had been a fierce warrior. I left my parents and joined the Queen.

"I found the King, he was cowering in what remains of his bedroom," said Katia.

"What should we do about him? It's his fault that all this happened. Imagine if we'd been taught at birth about ALL our powers, we never would have been in this position in the first place, " I told her angrily. "And what about what he did to poor Allie, locking her up like that. She could have died!"

"LOLA, he is his own worst enemy, his fear is like a prison. The best thing we can do is to educate the whole town on their special abilities and open their eyes to the big world out there waiting for them. If they are anything like you, they will learn quickly and they will all leave him far behind. He'll be left here all alone in the ruins of his Palace with no one to rule. Good luck to him," she told me calmly.

"But he has to pay for what he's done," I insisted.

"Don't you see? His greatest fears have come true, LOLA. He did all this for fear of losing his power and now it has all gone. All he has left are a load of old ruins. You will rebuild somewhere else and he will be left behind, believe me that is punishment enough for a power hungry King like him."

"I suppose you're right. If I wasn't so mad at him, I'd even feel a bit sorry for him," I ventured.

"That's my girl," Katia smiled, giving me a warm embrace. "You are a brave strong fairy and I am proud to call you my friend."

I smiled and I knew that she was right. The King no longer had any power over us, my friends and family were all safe and who can ask for more than that? We would rebuild, somewhere beautiful, where we could discover the true depths of our magical powers. Our people would learn from the mistakes of the King and this wisdom would keep us safe.

"There is only one thing left to do," I told the Queen.

"What's that LOLA?" she asked curiously.

"Why, throw a huge party of course!" I smiled. "Somehow we managed to get everyone out alive, and we need to thank the birds and the insects and the animals, without whom we couldn't have done this. And of course we need to thank you and the entire Water Fairy army!"

"I know a great DJ," said the Queen and she pointed over to Banjo.

"Banjo, really? I didn't know he was a DJ!" I replied giggling.

"Oh yes indeed, he is wicked on the decks, you have to see it to believe it."

What a night it was going to be.

THE END

And as the seasons come and go, here's something you might like to know. There are fairies everywhere: under bushes, in the air, playing games just like you play, singing through their busy day.

So listen, touch, and look around – in the air and on the ground. And if you watch all nature's things, you might just see a fairy's wing. *~ Author Unknown.*

ACKNOWLEDGEMENTS

This book was written whilst travelling through a number of beautiful locations, so I'd like to big up Saint Gervais, Lake Como, Provence, Amsterdam, Milan, Paris, London, Prague, Salzburg and Mallorca for providing me with the stunning views that inspired me to write a magical tale. Also, I'd be remiss if I didn't sing the praises of the beautiful Blue Mountains where Lola is set. I lived there for over a year and it is one of the most beautiful places on earth.

Super talented illustrator Craig Phillips brought Lola and her friends beautifully to life. It had to be you Craig, so thanks for fitting me in despite a crazy workload!

Thanks to my first readers and biggest supporters, Mum, Lee, Kim, Lana, Liam and Chloe for your most excellent advice and suggestions, your excitement and enthusiasm spurred me on. Special thanks to my Mum for always having a box of creative bits and pieces on hand when I was little and Blue Peter was my obsession (showing my age now), you fueled my inner creative beast and I'm grateful for it. Huge love to my little-big bro, I love you to the moon and back and thanks for bringing such amazing little people into the world.

I'm extremely lucky to have awesome friends who have supported me over the years, thanks for the advice and helpful suggestions along the way, but mostly for the love and the laughs. In alphabetical order, as I love you all dearly and will not pick favourites ☺ Chloe, Danny, Fudd, Gordon, Gwen, James, Jayne, Jo, Kate, Layto, Marnie, Nicki, Robyn, Seli, Shae, Sohan, Steve, Stu, Weave, Wendy, Will (Cate) and Will (Seddon).

Thanks to Reaya for helping me find a new path to follow.

Thanks to Seli for taking time off from living the dream to design my website and for making everything so simple, you rule.

Thanks to writers all over the world who inspire kids and adults to dream, question, challenge and be bold, my life has been enriched by your imagination and creativity.

Thanks to my second family, Mike and Cherry for always making me feel welcome and loved, superstar sister-in-law Charley, Malcolm, Rachel, Leo the lion and Millie the minx, Ross, Caroline and adorable Alice.

Saving the best for last, a million thanks to my husband Jem for too much to list here, you are my rock and my love always and forever.